TALES

From Around The

WOODSTOVE

(THE FIRST CUP OF COFFEE)

DEAN BURGESS

ARCHWAY
PUBLISHING

Archway Publishing books may be ordered through booksellers or by contacting:

Archway Publishing
1663 Liberty Drive
Bloomington, IN 47403
www.archwaypublishing.com
844-669-3957

ISBN: 978-1-6657-4107-1 (sc)
ISBN: 978-1-6657-4106-4 (e)

Library of Congress Control Number: 2023905537

Print information available on the last page.

Archway Publishing rev. date: 03/24/2023

Dedication

To my wife, who, like many wives, holds everything together. They are the true strength of families and the world.

Acknowledgments

To all those who have encouraged me over the years. The professors and students that encouraged me to write by saying they couldn't wait for the next paper. The professor who made me write a short story and read it in front of a crowd at a bookstore so that I could see other people's reactions to my writing. To those people there who cried while I read, know that your tears gave me the strength and courage to write. Thank you all.

01

*T*he elevator doors smoothly parted, and the man stepped out onto the third floor, three-year-old son on his hip, flanked by his eight-year-old daughter to his right, and his six-year-old daughter to his left. The nurse's station faced them, and the nurses behind the front desk, though busy, greeted them with a friendly "good morning" and a nod, joined by bright and cheerful smiles.

One of the nurses walked from behind the desk and in front of the waiting man and children. "Good morning, Wells family," she said cheerfully. "Are you ready for Christmas?" she said as her face scanned from the man and acknowledged each of the children. "How about you, Charlie?" she said. She leaned over and ruffled the little boy's hair.

"Yes! We saw Santa last night," he answered. He struggled to get down from his father's arms. It was one thing—and he had welcomed it—for his father to carry him from the parking lot, protecting him from traffic and the long trip up to the third floor. It was another matter altogether if someone was speaking to him, and his father was holding onto him like he was some sort of baby or something!

"You did? Well, that's great, Charlie!" the nurse said. She got down on her knees to speak eye to eye with the little boy. "Did you sit on his lap and tell him what you wanted for Christmas?" the nurse spouted cheerfully as she waited for the little boy's answer.

"A new red fire truck...and a puppy!" the boy bubbled.

"Well, that sounds just grand, Charlie!" the nurse answered. Next she slid along the floor in front of the little girl on the man's left.

"How about you, Beth?" the nurse questioned. "Did you tell Santa what you want for Christmas?"

"A new baseball mitt," the little girl answered. "And maybe an Easy-Bake Oven."

"Splendid!" the nurse responded. "I had an Easy-Bake Oven when I was a little girl."

The nurse quickly got on her feet to acknowledge the older sister. "How about you, Anna? What do you want for Christmas?"

Usually, Beth, the middle sister, was quiet. Anna was older, prim and proper, and ever respectful. She was not shy and easily engaged all those who spoke to her. Now, however, the weight of the situation before the family laid more heavily on Anna. She was eight and understood what the path forward likely meant. Anna was already becoming a protector of her two younger siblings.

"I just want my mom to be okay," she said stoically.

"Oh, I'm sure everything is going to be okay," the nurse answered cheerfully. In fact, she knew everything was *not* going to be okay. The nurse knew the grim prognosis of the little girl's mother. She also understood that the mother and father had told their children their mother, Katherine, was not going to make it, that soon she would be "joining Jesus in heaven."

Though all the children knew their mother was sick, Anna was the only one who understood the consequences of death and the fate awaiting their mother.

The nurse quickly stood in front of the man. "Now, if you need me to watch the children, we can go down to the cafeteria for a while so you can talk to her, and you two can be alone."

Mr. Wells nodded in recognition to the nurse at the task laying before him. "Thank you," he responded. "We will probably do that in a bit."

"Just let me know," the nurse answered as she walked back behind the desk to continue her duties.

"Let's go see Mom," the man said. He took the little boy's hand in his right hand, and Beth took his left hand. Anna took Charlie's hand in hers, and the family proceeded down the corridor. The smell of alcohol permeated the hallway. The heels of the family clicked and echoed on the cold, hard tiles.

Mr. Wells looked at the number on the door—room 29—and took a deep breath before entering. He silently prayed that this would be a good day for his wife. When she had entered the hospital, right after Thanksgiving, for what they both knew would be the final time, her goal was to make it to Christmas. Not only did she want to have one last Christmas with her family, but she wanted to make it a joyful one for the children, so that Christmas would never be a sad time for them, but a cheerful one.

Now, here we are, the day before Christmas. She made it, he thought. He was at once saddened, but also extremely proud of Katherine for being such a fighter. She had battled this heart-wrenching disease for two years now. She endured operations and sickness and treatments and tiredness and fatigue beyond comprehension of anyone who never had cancer. Yet she remained cheerful and hopeful because of her family. For the kids who needed a mom. For her husband, who needed a wife and companion. The man took a deep breath, gave a quick tap of his knuckles to alert anyone in the room, then turned the doorknob and stepped in, children in hand.

The woman, sitting up in bed, gave a cheerful "Hello! There's my family!" The children rushed to her side. Little Charlie propelled himself into the air toward the bed, and the waiting mother grabbed him, pulled him into the bed beside her, and kissed him. Beth also raced to the bed, sat on the edge, and leaned into the hugs and kisses of her mother. Anna walked to the far side of the bed, waiting her turn for an opening. She leaned forward into the waiting arms of her mother to join her brother and sister in Katherine's tender affections.

The man paused a couple of minutes to give his wife time with the kids. The woman reached one arm forward and motioned for the man to join then. He climbed onto the side of the bed and leaned in, kissing his wife, and joining the family in one all-embracing hug.

After an hour or so of the woman asking the children about home and their lives, and the children excitingly sharing their visit with Santa, the man could see his wife tiring. He slipped out of the room and asked the nurse if she could watch the kids for a few minutes. He returned to the room, followed by the nurse a couple of minutes later. The nurse asked the children to go with her for some special Christmas treats waiting for them in the cafeteria. The children then went with the nurse, leaving the man and his wife to themselves.

After a few minutes discussing the woman's health and what was going on in the kids" lives, the woman turned to her husband, looking him deep in the eyes. She had the ability to peer into his soul, and the man knew that. She could see parts of him no one else could see, and he had always loved that about her, even though he knew that look meant he was like putty in her hands.

The woman leaned forward. "David, how are you?" she asked. She took his hands into hers and continued to look deeply into his eyes.

"Fine," he said. "Just keeping busy with work."

"Honey, that's what I've been meaning to talk to you about—your work. I know you've worked hard and provided a great life for me and the kids but after I'm gone—"

The man quickly interrupted. "Gone? After you're gone? You're not going anywhere. You're going to get out of this hospital and come home with me and the kids, and everything will be—"

Now it was the wife's turn to interrupt her husband. She asserted a little more authority. "*After* I'm gone, the children are going to need you more than ever. I want you to pull back on your hours so you can be there for them. Maybe even move away from the city to a small town nearby. I always wanted to live in a small town, to raise the children there instead of running them to this event and that event every day. Just spend time with them away from the hustle and bustle of the city."

"Yes, but work. I have to work," the man said.

The woman leaned forward and kissed the man on the lips, the oxygen tube and tape underneath her nose pressing above his lips, stopping his protestations.

She looked deep into his eyes once again. "You have Ms. Fischer, the office manager. And you said that Tom Delaney was really sharp. I bet, if you tried, you could think of a way."

"Yes, but—" the man started to respond. The woman quickly put the tips of her fingers over the man's lips.

"Just think about it," the woman responded quietly. "That's all I ask. And maybe you could build a house out in the country some-place. I know the kids may miss their friends at first, but they'll adjust. They'll make new friends."

"Yes, but—." A small tear started to puddle in the man's eye. "Without you, how would I ever know where to build? You are always good at these things. I can't—"

The woman pressed her fingertips to the man's lips once again. "Shhhh. You'll know," she whispered. "You'll know."

The couple kissed and embraced once again. As they did, the raucous and excited crew of kids burst back into the room, followed by the smiling nurse. The children excitedly explained that Santa was in the cafeteria and had provided them treats. The nurse smiled and left the family alone to return to her work.

After a bit, the man noticed his wife tiring once again, and he urged the kids to say goodnight to their mom. "We have a big day tomorrow," he said.

After more kisses and embraces, the woman lay back in bed, saying goodnight to the children and her husband.

As the man gathered his crew and opened the door, an orderly stood before them, wearing a name tag of John B., his hand extended in front, about to knock. The man was deeply tanned, and his skin was heavily weathered. He wore a thick gray beard, and his eyes sparkled as he spoke.

"And how is Ms. Katherine today?" he asked cheerfully.

"A little tired, but she's had a good day," the husband answered.

"Well, I guess it's time to rejoice," the man answered with his deep, melodic voice that somehow soothed the husband.

The orderly made his way into the hospital room, and the husband then took the children in hand. They made their way back up the hallway and onto the elevator, retracing their steps of a couple of hours earlier.

02

*T*he man was awakened early by the sound of little feet running across the bedroom and jumping into his bed. Charlie and Beth and Anna had already peeked into the living room and found waiting presents under the tree and stockings filled with candy. From there, they all rushed into their father's room, exclaiming excitedly that Santa had come, and that their dad should come see. The temptation of just one more cuddle with their father was too great, however, and they all climbed into bed with the man and described what they had seen.

Soon, the call of their waiting treasures became too great, and they grabbed him by the hands and coaxed him out of bed. From there, the motley crew of pajama-clad soldiers trooped off into the living room, where they began to rip brightly colored paper, tossing it onto the floor in giant heaps. They gasped and awed and giggled at their finds.

There were various toys and a cowboy outfit, complete with hat, vest, star, holster, and silver cap pistol with a white handle for Charlie. He requested that his dad immediately load the pistol, and the crackle of caps soon followed, with outlaws falling behind sofa and tree.

Beth poured through her cadre of gifts, finding particular pleasure in her Easy-Bake Oven, complete with half a dozen or more of Easy-Bake cake mixes.

Anna made her way through various toys and clothes, finally spotting the professional art set that she had requested.

The children were thoroughly involved with their treasures when the father mentioned, "Oops! I believe there is one more for Charlie that we almost forgot."

After a few moments, the man made his way back to the living room, carrying a large box. He carefully set the box down onto the floor between the piles of toys.

"Charlie, I believe this is yours," said the man.

At that moment, the children were startled as the box began to move in starts.

"Well, aren't you going to open it?" the man asked Charlie as Anna and Beth closed in ranks around the box.

Charlie, with slight fear and trepidation, began to open the box. He slowly peeked inside as he pulled open the lid.

At once, all three children squealed in delight, "A puppyyyyyy!"

Charlie struggled to grasp hold of the waiting bundle of energy, and the girls helped him pry the furry creature from its confines. All three children took turns holding and playing with the animal, but it was particularly enamored with Charlie, perhaps proclaiming his newfound friend and partner in crime.

The father took a picture of the children with the new pup, and the crew excitedly dressed so that they could reveal to their mother the newfound treasures. They quarantined the pup in the kitchen to await their return. Each gathered a small, wrapped package that had been placed under the tree, bearing the handwritten title "Mom." The children gathered the gifts into their tiny hands and rushed to the car so they could get to the hospital to see their mother as soon as visiting hours allowed.

Once again, the man and children made their way along the cold, antiseptic corridor on the third floor. The man paused for a moment before opening the door, praying that his wife would be having another good day. He made a quick knock of warning before he slowly opened the door. The woman was sitting up in bed with a huge smile, holding out her arms. The children burst in once again, holding the gifts for their mother.

She grabbed Charlie and pulled him into bed beside her as she showered him with kisses, then Beth and Anna as they each took a place on each side of her. Her husband followed, giving her a big kiss and joining the group embrace.

"Before we go further," the woman explained as she pulled out a book from the stand beside the hospital bed, "your father has something to read." After handing her husband the book as he sat down on the chair beside her bed, she huddled the children close in bed beside her.

She had insisted that he always read the Christmas story on Christmas morning, starting when Anna was just a baby. She and the baby and the man huddled closely on the sofa near the fire and under the lights of the tree. As the family grew, the story and the tradition for the family remained the same. The hospital was not going to change that. Katherine was adamant on that point.

Afterward, the children started raucously explaining to their mother what Santa had brought, showing her the picture of the children and the new puppy.

The man smiled, as she looked surprised. His wife already knew what the dog looked like. She had spent the last few weeks searching pictures of puppies in kennels and those relegated to the nearby animal shelter, before finally deciding on just the right one for little Charlie.

The man had always objected to getting a dog because of the upkeep and the responsibility. Katherine was determined, after she entered the hospital for what she knew was likely to be the last time. "Every three-year-old boy needs a companion to grow up with," she argued to her husband.

The man relented, and Katherine had given him a big hug and kiss in reward on one of his hospital visits. A friend delivered the dog during the night as the children slept, and the man kept it a secret until the opening of the presents, just as his wife had planned.

As Charlie excitedly showed his mother the picture of the dog and children, his mother exclaimed to the little boy in approval, "Oh, how beautiful! What a champ. But what are you going to name him, Charlie?"

The little boy paused in deep contemplation for a few moments. "Hmmmm, I think that!" said Charlie, smiling.

The family all paused, trying to understand what Charlie was trying to tell them.

"Yes, what are you going to name him, Charlie?" repeated the woman.

Once again, Charlie repeated, "*That*! I'm going to name him Champ!"

The family erupted in approval. "Yes! Champ! That is an excellent name, Charlie!" agreed the woman, as the girls both voiced their agreement.

Then the children started handing their mother the presents each of them held in their tiny hands. The man smiled as he watched his wife act in wonder as to what each small box contained. The truth of the matter was that she had requested that the children make something by hand for her this year instead of the father trouping them to the store and letting the kids pick out presents.

She started with Charlie's gift first, shaking it as she said, "Ooohhh, I wonder what this is, Charlie?" This drew a proud smile from his lips. She tore the paper away and opened the box, revealing a handmade macaroni bracelet, painted all the colors of Christmas, by a three-year-old hand.

"Oh! It's beautiful, Charlie! Just what I was wanting!" she exclaimed as she immediately tied it around her wrist and held it out as if she was admiring a gift from Tiffany's.

Then Beth handed her mother her gift, as she smiled. Again, the mother shook the box as if to guess its contents. As the woman pulled back the paper and opened the box, it revealed a macaroni necklace, more neatly painted, but still the work of a child. "Oh, It's beautiful! It will go perfectly with my bracelet. Look!" the woman exclaimed as she placed the piece of fine art over her head, holding out her hand to show that it was a perfect accompaniment to the bracelet. Beth was pleased at the obvious appreciation of her mother for the fine treasure she had created.

Next, Anna timidly handed her mother the gift she had created. Once again, the mother excitedly shook the box as if to guess its contents, then slowly tore away the paper. She opened the box, revealing a hand-made pair of earrings, shaped as flowers, as well as a matching ring, all made from a home jewelry kit for kids. "Oh, how beautiful, Anna!" The woman exclaimed as she pinned the clip-on earrings to her lobes and place the ring on her finger. She held out the ring in admiration as if it was an expensive cocktail ring worth thousands of dollars. Anna smiled at the appreciation her mother exhibited for her handiwork.

The woman then pulled the children close and rewarded them with hugs and kisses, and the children reveled in the affection.

The man stood there, watched his family, and smiled, thankful that they had this time together. Somehow, the unending treatments and doctor's appointments and sickness and pain were all worth this one moment, this perhaps last time together. He was grateful for the strength and the determination his wife had shown.

"Now, I have a couple of gifts for you guys! Can you bring those gifts over here, honey?" She asked.

The man turned to the small tree on the table in the corner of the room. It was against hospital policy; the staff had adamantly protested. Nevertheless, after Katherine had remained so steadfast, the doctors finally relented when she had threatened that she would spend Christmas at home if she couldn't have a small tree to share with her family. The family had spent a day together in her hospital room and played Christmas music and they decorated the tree, just as had become a little tradition that the woman had insisted upon.

"This one says, "To: Charlie. From: Mom,'" the man said as he handed the gift to the little boy as he lay in the hospital bed in his mother's arms.

The little boy excitedly took the package in his small hands and began to hurriedly tear at the wrapping. With wide eyes, a large smile, and joyful voice he shouted "firetruck" as he revealed the prize. "Oh! Thank you, Mommie!" he gushed as he pressed himself close inside his mother's arms and she showered him with hugs and kisses.

As they did this, and the little boy drove his new toy over the covers and pillows, the man gathered up the scraps of brightly colored paper, placed them into the wastebasket against the wall, and gathered another present from beneath the small Christmas tree.

"Let's see. Now, Beth!" he said as he handed the next package to her. She smiled and accepted it. She began to feel its odd shape through the paper. As she did, the man said, quizzically, "I wonder what that could be?" and glanced quickly at his wife. They both smiled at each other.

The man knew what it was. As much as he had protested and tried to coax his daughter into liking tea parties and frilly dresses, she had wanted a baseball mitt. His wife had insisted that the child be allowed to follow her own drummer, and the father relented. How could he not? His wife was insisting on it from what was almost certainly the last Christmas she would spend with her daughter. "Well, you are always right about these things, anyway." The man smiled at his wife as he agreed. She rewarded the man with a huge kiss. The man delivered the present and paper to his wife's hospital room one day before the children were out of school for Christmas vacation. Katherine had insisted she be allowed to wrap the gifts herself; and so, it was: the man watching with a smile on his face as the woman wrapped the children's gifts, small tears occasionally welling in her eyes.

"A baseball mitt!" the little girl squealed as she quickly placed it on one hand while she tightened her other hand into a ball and pounded it into the mitt. "Oh, thank you, Mom!" she said as she burrowed against her mother closely and kissed her on the cheek again and again.

The man gathered the scraps of paper once again, tossed them into the wastebasket, then quizzically looked under the tree. "Hmm. One more," the man said. "I wonder who this could be for. Let's see. It says, "To: Anna. From: Mom."" He took the present in his hands and handed it to his oldest daughter as she patiently sat on the bed with her mother.

Anna smiled as she gratefully took the present from her father and looked with appreciative eyes towards her mother. Instead of ripping through the paper as the other two children had done, Anna daintily unwrapped her gift and folded up the remains. "Oh! My own makeup kit!" She exclaimed as she grabbed her mother and traded hugs and kisses.

Again, the husband looked into the eyes of his wife as she tenderly hugged their daughter. The man had objected to makeup for a daughter, who seemingly wanted to grow up a lot faster than he wanted to allow. Again, the man had relented and purchased the gift at the direction of his wife. He watched while she wrapped it, tears welling and lips smiling.

"Now I have one for you," the man said as he looked at his wife, pulling a small, neatly wrapped package from the pocket of his sports coat.

"Oh! I wonder what it is?" she said as she playfully shook the gift, listening for any sounds.

The woman then carefully unwrapped the gift and opened a small box. "Oh look," she said, "two rubies for me and your father, and a diamond for each of my precious children: one for Anna, one for Beth, and one for Charlie. It's beautiful!" she exclaimed, with a large smile as she proudly pinned the brooch to her hospital gown.

She motioned for her husband, and the group joined once more for kisses and a warm hug.

"And I have one for you, David. It should be here any moment. But could you ask the nurse to take the kids down to the cafeteria for a few minutes first?" she asked her husband.

"Sure, dear," he answered. "Okay, kids, let's see if one of the nurses can take you down to the cafeteria for a few minutes."

The children took turns hugging their mother, then held hands with their father once again and made their way down to the nurse's station. One of the nurses agreed to take the children down to the cafeteria for a few minutes. While they were gone, the man returned to his wife's room, where he found her sitting up in bed once again. She motioned for him to sit on the bed beside her, and he did.

Katherine took her husband's hand into hers and looked into his eyes. "Now, dear, I know things are going to be difficult without me," she began.

The man quickly interrupted. "Without you? You're not going anywhere. You're going to be out of this place and home before you know it. And then we are—"

The woman stopped him by placing her fingertips over his lips and whispering, "Shhhhh, shhhhhh. It's okay. I love you and the children with all my heart, and I am grateful for the time we have had together. I don't want you to worry. When you need me most, I will be there."

The woman recognized the denial the man had faced ever since she had been first diagnosed. They both had fought this illness. But while she had gradually been able to face the inevitable conclusion, he had simply been unable to face any thoughts of a life without her. She knew it was crushing him, that he was trying to remain strong for her and the kids, and he was unable to face the coming days.

Her greatest wish and her greatest prayer since she had entered the hospital the weekend after Thanksgiving was that she would be able to make this one last Christmas a happy one for her husband

and her kids. She wanted future Christmases to be a time of hope and joy instead of one of death and despair. She had reached down and gathered all her strength and energy she had left to make it a happy one. Now, she could feel the strength begin to drain from her body. She only had to give her husband, her family, this one last gift. The woman softly kissed the man on his lips and held him once again.

"Now, dear, I have one last gift to give you and the kids. And I know you are going to want to say no at first, but I want you to give this at least a try. For me?" she asked.

"Yes," he said. "Whatever it is."

As the man spoke those words, they both heard a knock on the door.

"Mrs. Wells?" came a voice from the hallway.

Katherine took her husband's hand in hers as she cheerfully answered. "Yes, come in."

The door slowly opened and a cheerful woman of about fifty came into the room, smiling.

"Hello, Katherine," the woman said as she made her way into the room. "Am I too early?"

"No. In fact, I would say this was perfect timing," the wife said as she smiled.

"Dear, this is someone I want you to meet. This is Melba Anderson. Melba is going to be your new live-in housekeeper."

The man shook the woman's hand. "Hello, Melba," he said. He then turned with a questioning look at his wife.

"Dear," Katherine began, "I have interviewed at least thirty people. And Melba is perfect. She lost her husband and little girl in a car wreck a long time ago and has never remarried. I think Melba is the woman we need, and we are the family she needs."

"But—" the man started, and the woman quickly placed her finger against his lips.

"Remember, you promised you would at least give it a try. This is my gift to you and the kids—perhaps, my last gift to you and the kids. At least give it a try?" she said.

The man smiled and relented. "Yes, at least a try." He then turned to Melba. "Well, looks like we have a new housekeeper."

The woman smiled at the man and then at his wife.

Katherine said, "So I guess it's time to introduce you to the kids. Can you bring them in now, dear?"

The man left the room and returned in a few minutes with the children. The man and woman then introduced the woman to their kids. They each seemed immediately comfortable with her, and the couple explained that Miss Melba would be living with them and helping around the house.

The family spent several more hours together, letting the children get at ease with the woman and the woman at ease with the children. Later, as Katherine began to tire, the family gave her a huge hug and many kisses and excused themselves so she could rest. The family left to make arrangements for the newest member of their family, to retrieve her luggage and personal items, and move her into the guest bedroom right off the kitchen in their house.

03

*T*he man rode the elevator to the third floor of the hospital, as he had every day since just after Thanksgiving. The girls were holding each of his hands. This time, however, rather than holding Charlie in his arms, or having him exert his independence by running in front of the family, Charlie was in the arms of the new housekeeper/family member, Melba. The children loved the additional attention that Melba provided them, and she loved caring for a family again.

As the elevator reached the third floor, revealing the familiar nurse's station and crew of busy nurses, Charlie, once again, wanted to exert his independence and show the nurses just how grown up he was. The family stepped off the elevator, and the nurses, once again, as they had done daily for the last month, acknowledged their familiar visitors with friendly nods and hellos. The all-too-familiar clicks of heels filled the hallway, along with the heavy antiseptic smell of alcohol.

The father softly rapped his knuckles against the door and the family cheerfully flooded the room. This time, however, instead of the mother sitting upright in bed and smiling as she awaited her family with open arms, the woman lay quietly still. The sound of the beeping heart monitor filled the room. Slowly, the woman opened her eyes, sensing the presence of her family. The woman slowly raised her body to a sitting position and smiled. Charlie ran to the bed and jumped towards his mother's waiting arms. This time, however, she no longer had the strength to pull him into bed beside her. The man quickly closed ranks and helped his son into the bed beside his mother. The two girls joined their mother and brother, softly sitting on each side of the bed. The mother then grabbed the children and pulled them close. As she did, the familiar wave of her hand to join them ensued, and the family kissed and embraced.

After a few moments, the woman turned her attention to Melba, standing and smiling at the loving family before her. Katherine smiled at the woman and said, "Hello, Melba. Did you get started moving in? And did they treat you okay?"

Melba stepped forward and grasped Katherine's outstretched hand with hers. "Yes! Of course! You have a lovely family. And I made breakfast early. Charlie's favorite, pancakes and eggs. At least that's what he told me."

Katherine smiled and chuckled lightly. "I think you are going to find that Charlie has lots of favorites."

As the man watched the two women talk, he was startled by how quickly his wife's health had deteriorated. Her skin had become ashen, and the cheerful smiles she had presented as Christmas approached had become strained and forced. Her voice trembled at times as she spoke to Melba and the children. Occasionally, the man noticed a slight grimace of pain on the face of his wife before she forced another smile.

He recalled how his wife's wish was that she would make it through yesterday, to have one last happy Christmas with her children. She wanted a Christmas the family could cherish. She had accomplished that, he thought. It might have taken everything she had, but she accomplished that. He was proud of his wife and loved her deeply, not just for their marriage and the children and the memories they had made together. Now, more than ever, he appreciated her strength and determination.

As they day wore on, the woman asked that the children be allowed, one at the time, into her room. She started with Anna. She hugged and kissed her, and told her how proud of her she was and how beautiful she was. She recalled to her the day she was born and how she had thought she was the most beautiful child in the world when she first saw her face.

The mother had made sure that Anna brought her makeup kit with her, and they spent their time alone together applying makeup to each other and talking. As their time together drew to a close, she told Anna to take care of her father and brother and sister, and to make sure Melba would feel as if she was family. The two embraced softly and quietly, and the mother told her daughter how much she loved her.

Likewise, when Beth joined her mother for their time alone, the mother recounted the girl's birth, how beautiful she was, and how proud she was of her. The two softly tossed a baseball into the new Christmas present Beth had received from her mother. Beth sat on the edge of the bed as her mother tenderly brushed her hair, and the daughter was reminded to take care of her sister, brother, and father and to make sure Melba felt like family. They talked about baseball cards and boys until it was time for Charlie to come in. The woman and the daughter shared a tender embrace, and the woman told her how much she loved her.

Next, Charlie burst into the room, carrying his new firetruck. The man helped his son into bed beside his wife and excused himself, leaving the two alone. Charlie was thrilled and filled with pride as his mother told him of the day of his birth. She explained to him that she had never seen a more handsome baby. As they drove the toy firetruck and miniature cars over the makeshift roadways of the bed linen, she reminded the little boy to be strong and take care of his father and sisters, and to look after Melba because she needed a family to care for.

Next, the woman called the husband and then Melba into her room, where she quietly consulted with each. Afterwards, the entire family returned to the room together. It was obvious the woman was tired, so the man invited the children to say goodnight to their mom. She hugged them and kissed them. As each kissed her and said goodnight, the mother told each one that she loved them and told them goodbye.

Their quiet time together was pierced by the hospital paging system. "To all our guests, this is your second notice, visiting hours are over. Please exit now. Dr. Moab, please dial extension four twenty-two."

"Well, I guess that is our cue. Goodnight, Katherine," the man said.

The woman smiled at her family through misty eyes. "Goodbye. I love you all."

The man and Melba loaded the family up in the car and they quietly drove home. The children were exhausted and dozing. The man was quiet as he drove through the spits of snow beginning on the cold winter night. He was haunted by the "goodbye" of his wife. She had always smiled, even on her worst days in the hospital, told the family goodnight, and that she would see them tomorrow.

Upon arriving home, the man coaxed the children into their pajamas, and kissed the children goodnight. It was a terrible night of sleep for the man, but finally exhaustion hit him as sleep overtook him, as restless as it was.

It was seven in the morning, and the phone pierced the quietness. The hospital called and told the man that his wife had taken a turn for the worse and that he should get there as quickly as possible. The man woke his housekeeper. Together, they quickly dressed and then placed winter coats over the pajama-clad children as they placed them into the car. From there, the family fought the growing snowfall across town and raced into the hospital.

Upon arriving on the third floor, the nurses tried to stop the family, but they rushed to the woman's room and opened the door.

There, the family saw the woman still and peaceful. All the tubes that had helped her sustain life had been removed.

The woman, sensing the night before after her family left that the time was near for her, had made the nurses promise that they wouldn't allow her family to see her in distress. She instructed the nurses that she wanted the tubes removed. She wanted the macaroni bracelet and necklace and the pin representing her family be put on her. Her lips were to hold the lavender lipstick that she and her oldest child had shared together over Christmas.

As the family stepped inside the door, a nurse quickly followed. "I'm sorry," she said. "I tried to stop you at the desk but you were too quick. She passed away just a little while ago."

The man nodded and reassured the nurse that it was okay. The children each said their goodbyes to their mother and kissed her on the cheek. Melba then took the children down to the cafeteria to allow the man time with his wife. He told her through teary eyes that he loved her and asked her how she expected them to survive without her. He kissed his wife goodbye, then stepped out into the hallway.

He looked out of the window into the breaking light of day and through the softly falling snow. His vision was interrupted by a glint of red in the corner of his eye. There, huddled on the ledge, was a cardinal, flicking the snow piling up on the ledge of the building with its beak. The man smiled through tears that rolled down his cheeks as he watched the bird. Soon, the bird flew off into the falling snow. He made arrangements with the nurses and then joined his waiting family in the cafeteria. They all got into the car for their trip back across town through the softly falling snow. Two days later, the woman was buried wearing her prized macaroni jewelry, a pin with jewels denoting her family, and wearing makeup and lavender colored lipstick.

04

*O*ver the next month, the family started to return to normal as best they could. The girls returned to school, Charlie returned to daycare, and Melba began to take her place as a member of the family. The children instantly liked her, and she gave them kind and loving care, along with fulfilling her duties as live-in housekeeper. The man returned to work and the long hours to which he had become accustomed.

Though Melba filled in for their mother as best she could, the man become overwhelmed with work and rushing to the various extracurricular functions in which the children were involved. He made it a point to try to be there for his kids, but, with work, it was sometimes impossible. Melba, however, filled in the gaps wonderfully, and she made sure that someone was always there for the children.

It was late January, a month after his wife had died, and the man found himself on a business trip in Charlotte, away from Atlanta. Anna had a school play, and the man was trying to get back to Atlanta to be there for her. A winter storm had set in, however, and flights from Charlotte to Atlanta had been cancelled. The man decided to rent a car and try to make it back to Atlanta in time for his little girl's play that evening. If he was lucky, and the weather held, he should be home in time to see his little girl and the play that she so dearly wanted him to be there for.

As he drove, the weather gradually became worse, and eventually the interstate between Charlotte and Atlanta was closed. The rental car was luckily equipped with a GPS, and a quick reroute command saw the man navigating the mountainous roads on his way home. Soon, however, the man became lost, and his fuel began to run low. After desperately hoping to find some place to stop for gas, or perhaps locate a familiar road, the man saw a small set of buildings at an intersection of two roads. "Caughman's Store" read one of the signs, and it had two gas pumps proudly standing in front.

The man pulled up next to the pumps. There was no place to swipe his credit card. The man, however, pulled the hose and nozzle from its stand, cranked a handle on the side of the pump that set the amount of gas back to zero. Magically, the pump whirred, and he could see and feel the gas begin to rush from the pump into his car. He smiled and then cackled to himself that such an old-fashioned pump still existed.

After filling his tank, the man slowed the gas to a trickle and was able to stop exactly at forty dollars. He then placed the nozzle back in its cradle and made his way to the front of the old structure. He walked through the falling snow and up the steps. A screened door with a large Sunbeam Bread sign and picture of a little girl eating a sandwich was painted onto the screen. The man slowly coaxed the door open, and it squeaked, almost melodically, as he did. He then twisted the doorknob of the old front door and stepped inside.

The old country store was a cornucopia of goods stacked on tables and racks and on the various counters around the store. While neatly kept, it was eye-opening to see the sheer volume of goods in one small store. There were racks of coveralls, work pants, and other clothing dotting the central spaces. Canned goods and grocery items sat on shelves along the left and back walls. In the far-right corner was a large sign that read "Feed and Seed." Behind a counter was a large opening that led to a back room

As the man's eyes travelled farther along the right wall, he saw a group of men on wooden chairs huddled around an old pot-bellied stove. The stove gave off warmth that the man could feel instantly as he stepped just inside the front door. To his right was another counter with a sign hanging over it that read "Meats and Cheeses."

As the man was trying to take it all in, a voice behind a counter just to his left asked, "Can I help you, sir?"

As his attention adjusted, he noticed the store clerk behind the counter, a man in his fifties with dark hair that was graying slightly. The figure was stocky, but with strong arms that belied years of toil.

"Yes. I got some gas," the man said.

The older gentleman asked, "How much?"

"Uhmmm, forty dollars," the younger man answered.

The storekeeper rung up forty dollars on the old cash register, pressed another button with his finger, and a loud "ding" erupted from the old machine. The cash drawer flew open.

"Uhm, aren't you going to check the amount on the pump or anything?" the younger man asked quizzically.

"Why? Don't you know how much you got?" asked the store clerk.

"Yes. I just thought—" the younger man's voice trailed off. He was unaccustomed to the amount of trust shown to a customer when there were obviously no electronic gauges inside to show the clerk the amount that the man had pumped.

"Nevermind," the younger man said, relenting to the older man's trust that he had shown. "It sure is cold out. Do you have any hot coffee for sale?" He handed the older gentleman two twenty-dollar bills. The man took the money, placed it into the old cash register, and it rang once again, tallying the purchase.

"Well, we don't have any hot coffee for sale, but we always keep a pot on that stove right there," the clerk replied, pointing to the woodstove the older men sat around. "You are more than welcome to a cup."

"Thanks. Are you sure you won't let me pay you something for it?" the younger man asked.

"No. The first cup is free to strangers and anyone that may need to be warmed. More than that, and there is a coffee tin back there on the shelf by the cups. People will generally throw a little money in, and that keeps the coffee going for all," the older man said.

"Well, thank you then," the man relented. He smiled as he thought about the quaint whimsy of the situation. He walked toward the old stove and the group of old men near it.

"Howdy," one of the caretakers of the old stove said as the younger man stepped near them, having overheard the conversation between the younger man and the clerk. The other three men joined in their own greetings, from "hello" and "how are you" to a comment about how cold the weather was.

"It sure is," said the younger man as he tried to orient himself.

"There's mugs on that shelf right there, if you want to warm yourself by the fire a bit," said one man as he nodded invitingly to one of the wooden chairs by the fire.

"Well, I kind of need to be getting back home, if I can," answered the younger man.

"I see," said one of the older gentlemen, almost disappointed over not having a new guest at their gathering. "Well, in that case, there are some paper cups right next to that coffee tin there."

The younger man reached for one of the paper cups stacked on a small shelf next to the wall. Beside it, he saw a tin with various denominations of bills and change. He smiled as he thought about the honor system coffee in the old store. He separated one of the paper cups from the stack and stepped toward the coffee pot on top of the pot-bellied stove.

"Pretty dangerous roads in this weather. You got far to go?" asked one of the men, in a kind voice.

"Well, I'm trying to get back to Atlanta so I can get to my little girl's program at school tonight, if they have it," said the young man. "All the flights out of Charlotte to Atlanta were cancelled, so I got a rental and decided to drive. Then they closed the interstates, so here I am."

"Well, at least warm your bones for a couple of minutes," said one of the older gentlemen.

"Okay. Maybe just a minute," answered the younger man. He poured a trail of coffee into a paper cup, and then sat down on one of the wooden chairs. As he did, the older men continued with the stories that they had been exchanging. Laughter punctuated at regular intervals, and even the younger man found his jaws hurting from the smiles brought forth to him by the kind, older men with warm, whimsical eyes as they spun their yarns.

The minute or two that the man had intended to warm himself had quickly turned into twenty. The man looked at his watch.

"I'm sorry. But I need to get on the road." The young man tried to excuse himself.

The older men answered with well wishes of safety and luck and hopes of better weather for the younger man's trip. The young man tossed his empty paper cup into the small trashcan beside the door. He braced himself for the cold as he stepped out of the door and listened once again to the loud, melodic squeak of the screened door.

The blowing snow had piled onto his car in the short time he had been inside. As he neared his car, the man's attention fastened on a cardinal shimmying and tossing bits of snow into the air with its bright yellow beak. The man's mind rewound to the morning of his wife's death only a month before and the cardinal clinging to the side of the building and tossing the drifted snow into the air.

The man carefully watched the bird as he slowly approached the car, not wanting to scare the bird away but to catch more of its beauty. He was able to make it to within a couple of feet of the car, silently watching as the bird returned its gaze. Suddenly, the bird flew from the hood of the car and onto a wooden sign by the highway. It advertised 100.22 acres, and had a large red arrow pointing to a side road, a phone number, and the name of a real estate company.

The man stood still as he watched the bird on the sign looking at him for a couple of minutes. Suddenly, the bird flew off. The man turned back to the store and opened the squeaking door once again. He stepped into the warmth of the store and asked the clerk, "Say, is that land on that sign still for sale?"

"Well, I reckon it is," answered the clerk. "That is down by the judge's place. Judge, that McEntyre place down by you still for sale?"

The younger man made his way back to the group of older men once again.

"Well, you want it to live on, young fella?" They've been wanting to sell it to a big developer. Is it just you and your wife or—?"

The younger man interrupted. "No. My wife just recently passed away. It would be me and my three children, and a housekeeper," he added.

"Well, I tell you what. Tom Storey out at the real estate office is handling that land for a developer. You tell him you want them to throw in that twenty acres of bottom land into the deal too. I know it ain't worth much "cause it's mostly swamp, but it will keep the big developers out. I would be proud to have you and your family as neighbors. If you need any help with Tom, you tell him Judge Long sent you. Here is my number. If you need anything at all, you just let me know." The older man wrote his name and number down on a slip of paper and handed it to the younger man.

"Well, thank you so much, Mr.—." The younger man paused as he shook the older man's hand, not knowing how to address him.

"Long," answered the older man. "Rupert Long. But you can just call me Judge if you like. Everyone else does."

"Well, thank you very much, Judge Long. I will give this real estate agent a call and we will see where this goes," said the younger man.

The two men smiled at each other, and the younger man excused himself once again before opening the squeaking door. He stepped outside. The snow had stopped, and the sun was breaking through the clouds, quickly warming the air. The man then copied the information displayed on the sign onto the piece of paper the judge had given him. He climbed back into his rental car and began to drive, no longer chilled by the cold wind and the snow, but warmed by the sun and the old country store.

05

Over the next few months, the man closed on the property with the help of Judge Long. The design of the house for the family had been approved, and construction began in earnest. The children were sad about leaving their friends and school behind. Their father and Melba, their loving housekeeper, repeatedly assured them that they would make new friends and that a great adventure awaited them all.

It took some convincing by the father and children for Melba to be persuaded to make the move. However, the teary eyes of the children and the father's statement that the housekeeper was now family and severely needed worked magic on the housekeeper's heart. The truth was, the man and the children had become family to her as well, and she needed them every bit as much as they needed her.

David Wells had promoted Tom Delaney to operations manager and had given even more authority to Mrs. Fischer as office manager. The man's new house would include a large office and a conference room, if needed. With any luck, he would be able to keep office trips to Atlanta and sales trips to a minimum. He would now be able to spend more time with his children, just the way Katherine had planned.

As construction progressed, he loaded his little family up in the car and they proceeded to spend Saturdays together, watching the progress on their new house and exploring the land and surrounding area. The man bought hammers for the children, and they would spend time hammering boards, taking some comfort in having even a small hand in the building of their new home.

On one trip, after the walls had been framed and each child's room had been located, the father noticed Charlie placing a framed picture of his mother between the boards where they told him that his bed would be located.

"What are you doing, Charlie?" the man asked, while the girls and housekeeper looked on in curiosity.

"I'm putting a picture of Mom in the wall where my bed is going to be so she can always be with us, Dad," the little boy said proudly.

The man smiled, and he noticed the housekeeper smiling as well at the touching moment.

"I think that's a great idea, Charlie!" said the man. "How about you, girls? Would you like to do the same to your rooms?"

"Yes!" the girls screamed in unison.

"Well, they are supposed to hang sheetrock this week. I'll tell you what. I'll call the builder and have him leave a place in the walls where your beds are going to be. You can bring a picture of Mom and place it in the wall, just like Charlie. Would that be okay?" he asked.

"Yes!" the girls said.

And so it was. The builder left an area in the walls where the children's beds would be placed. The next weekend, the father, children, and housekeeper made their pilgrimage to their new home at Crabapple Creek. Three pictures of their mother were sealed forever in the place the children would grow and lay their heads at night.

The school year came to a close, and the new home was completed during the summer. A moving van was called, and boxes were loaded carefully. The little family said goodbye to their school and friends and hello to their new life.

06

David Wells decided to take a break from his morning routine. The kids were at school, and Melba was busily cleaning the house before the hurricane of three kids returning from school made some tasks virtually impossible. He pushed himself away from his desk and began to take the two-mile walk along the old country road towards Caughman's Store. David passed fields and pastures with cows and horses. By a stretch of woods, he paused as a deer with two yearlings, still showing their spots, slowly meandered across the quiet road in front of him.

Finally, he reached the little country store and listened as the screen door made its melodic announcement when he slowly pulled it open and stepped inside. He smiled and gave a quick hello to McCoy, the store owner, before turning his gaze toward the group of old men gathered around the quaint woodstove that held the familiar pot of coffee.

As David gathered a Styrofoam cup and began to pour, the men interrupted their storytelling and jokes to wish David a happy good morning. There was Judge Long, who had helped David expedite the closing on the property earlier in the year. Judge Long was an elderly man in his seventies, with a quick wit and wonderfully dry sense of humor. His white hair gave him an air of distinction, even as the twinkle in his eyes made you smile, warning you that humor and mischief weren't far away.

In the wooden slatted chair next to Judge Long sat Henry Thomas. Hank was the name of familiarity he often answered to for those that knew him best. As David learned from McCoy on his weekly visits to check on things as his new home was being built, Hank's father had passed away when he was in the third grade, leaving the family scrambling for money to make ends meet. Hank had procured a job sweeping floors at the local textile mill, and eventually worked his way up to factory manager. He took night school classes for his GED and eventually took classes at a nearby college. Though Hank held his own to match the humor of his friends, his soft voice made everyone feel at ease and foretold of the kindness within. With gray hair and a soft smile, Hank made everyone feel warmth and comfort.

Next to Hank sat Doc Holley. Also in his seventies, Doc Holley presented a little more-stately manner, but with the same warmth and humor prevalent in his small group of friends. Doc Holley somehow looked familiar to David, but he could never quite put his finger on where or how.

Bringing up the far end of the group was Stan Nichols. Stan was the farmer of the bunch, and, except for having served in the military, had lived in the community all his life. He never strayed very far, except on vacations to visit family members who had decided to seek their fortunes in faraway places. Stan matched the others in age and hair color, but his hands, arms, and weather-worn face made it apparent that he was used to the outside and manual labor of a farmer's life. Stan's kind eyes and great smile, however, made him fit right in with the rest of his friends gathered around this old woodstove in this small country store.

As much as David wanted a cup of coffee and a break from his work, it was the company of this older band of gentlemen and their warm tales and humorous stories that he had come in search of. As he listened to the jokes and stories, David watched as Judge Long would ponder one of the other men's tales, working a small wooden figure through his fingers as he listened.

Soon, however, as was his custom, Judge Long removed an old penknife and small block of wood from his pocket. He began to peel thin slivers from the wedge, letting them fall to the floor at his feet. As he transformed the wooden block, he held a pipe between his teeth. Little rings of sweet-smelling cherry tobacco smoke dissipated and worked their way among the jokes and tall tales.

As David watched the old sage ply his craft, he noticed other small figures of animals sitting on a nearby shelf among the plentitude of goods. Curiosity finally got the better of the younger man. He asked, "Judge, did you carve all of those?"

"Well, I reckon so," the Judge answered. "Not a whole lot to do when you get my age other than sitting around telling stories and gnawing on a piece of hickory wood."

"Those are great!" exclaimed the younger man. "How did you learn to carve?"

"Well, I guess it reminds me of a story, one of a little boy, perhaps nine or ten. He'd spend his days in the front yard of the small house his family had out at town, tossing a baseball in the air, catching it with an old mitt. The youngster would toss the ball into the air, circumvent his yard, and nab it the best he could while waiting for his father to come home from work. The father being an attorney, his days were long, and the boy's waiting was often for naught, as the father wouldn't make it into the driveway until well after dark.

"Often, while waiting, the young lad would hear the cheerful and melodic whistle of an old vagrant who would pass the little house on the way into town to purchase whatever food the old man could afford at the Piggly Wiggly. Sometimes, the man would stop various neighbors and ask them if he could perhaps perform little odds and ends jobs, such as rake leaves or trim bushes, to raise a little cash for food. His whistles always fascinated the youngster, as they preceded the march of this unkempt, little old man with shaggy hair, and beard to match, into and out of town.

"One day, curiosity about this old gentleman got the better of the youngster. The boy climbed onto his bike and followed the itinerant down the streets and through the outskirts of town, keeping well back to not alert the old man that he was being followed. The old gentleman finally disappeared into the woods down there at Steadman's Pond. The younger fellow stealthily searched for the older, being careful to guard his presence, but was unable to locate the old man.

"The boy was unable to get much sleep during the night, as his curiosity about the old guy had gotten the better of the lad. He lay awake for hours, pondering what could have happened to the old man. The boy made up his mind to solve the mystery. The next day, he made his way on his bike to Steadman's Pond. He slowly drove over the dam and past the spillway, looking for signs of the old guy. With no sign of him, the youngster made his way on his bike into the brambles, and onto a footpath. From there, deep in the woods, he could see an old structure, constructed from sheets of old plywood and two-by-fours and other various scraps that had obviously been discarded at the nearby trash pile.

"The fortress wasn't much larger than a small toolshed. It had one window with broken glass that was covered by a sheet of plastic. The door was no more than a bunch of wood nailed together and fastened with old, rusty hinges over a small frame. The boy slowly opened the door, prepared to run as fast as he could to his nearby bicycle and quickly peddle back into town. But the place was empty. All that he could see was an old wooden table and chair, and a small woodstove similar to this one. One of the cast-iron legs had broken off, and it was propped up in that corner with several old bricks. On one wall, a board was nailed, forming a shelf, with little figurines of animals lining it.

"The young lad became worried that the old man might come back and accuse him of trespassing, so he quietly left the old cabin. Still curious as to where the old man might be, he walked back through the woods and parked his bicycle along the path. He continued through the woods a piece until he heard someone singing in a beautiful Irish brogue.

"'In Scarlet town where I was born
There was a fair maid dwelling
And every youth cried well away
For her name was Barbara Allen."

"He had a beautiful voice that resonated over the water and deep into the woods. As he followed the sound to the edge of the pond, he could see the old man fishing and singing in the far corner of the pond. The boy watched for a while but became startled by the rustling wings of an owl, the twilight overtaking him. His heart pounding at the owl and concerned about his parents worrying about him for coming home after dark, he rushed back through the woods and hopped on his bike, quickly peddling his retreat.

"However, his pants leg got caught in the chain. This caused the chain to derail and get caught in the teeth of the cog, breaking the chain in two and jamming it tightly in the cogs. He managed to extricate his pants, but the bike was unable to move. It was locked tight. The boy decided that discretion was the wise choice. He left his bike against that old tree and made his way through the woods and back home.

"He was afraid to tell his parents about his adventure and the old man. After a sleepless night, the next day he made his way down the street, to the outskirts of town, and into the woods at Steadman's Pond. Still scared, he retraced his steps to the old tree where he left his bike. There, instead of the tangled mess of chain and cog, he found the old bike had been repaired. The chain was untangled and in place, held together by a piece of wire. He made his way back through the woods and back home, keeping what had happened a secret, fearing punishment for following that old man into the woods.

"In the days that followed, the young boy would watch the old man whistling as he travelled up the street and into town, followed by his return trip, sometime later, back toward Steadman's Pond. Occasionally, the young boy would return on his bicycle, watching and listening to the old man singing as he fished across the pond. He never acknowledged the boy watching, and the young boy was too scared to approach the old itinerant.

"As the long days of summer stretched into the crisp fall, and the leaves began to turn, the boy continued his trips into the woods of Steadman's Pond, listening to that old man sing. As Christmas approached, the young lad thought of that old man, alone in the woods, and wrapped up an old sweater his father had put in the Salvation Army bin. He wrapped it, grabbed a couple of cans of food out of the pantry, and left it all by the old tree on Christmas Eve.

"The day after Christmas, he rode his bike back into the woods at Steadman's Pond and to the tree where he had left the presents. Gone were the sweater and canned goods. In their place was a small package made of brown grocery paper and tied together with a vine from the woods. He opened it and found a carving, similar to this small robin you see me keep in my pocket.

"Over the years, the boy continued to leave canned goods from his pantry, or clothes his father was discarding, by the old tree. In their place, each time he would find another package with another hand-carved figure.

"Sometimes, the boy would see the old man wearing one of those old sweaters or shirts as he made his way, whistling through town. Sometimes, the young boy would return to the pond and watch the old man singing across the cool waters of the lake. Other than a quick smile when he saw the young boy in town, the old man never acknowledged him, and the boy never acknowledged the old man to his parents, for fear they would punish him for following that old, crusty man to Steadman's Pond.

"Their exchange of gifts continued until the young boy went off to college. He even brought those old carvings with him, placing them in his dorm room to remember those moments of watching that old man across Steadman's Pond. When he returned home at Christmas, he brought gifts and food for the old man. When he went to place them by the old tree, he found a package wrapped with the same old vine and brown paper lying there. He opened it, and it was an old penknife. He searched the pond and cabin for the old man, but he was gone. The rustic shelter was falling in and there was nothing there.

"During Christmas, the boy attended church with his family. There, he listened as the old women in flowered dresses and beautiful hats talked among themselves about that old man. Some of the women called him a vagrant. Some said it was good riddance he was gone. Some said he had once been a successful businessman but had lost his daughter and wife in a car accident and was never the same. One woman said that she thought he might have been an angel, but the other women laughed at her. The boy had no idea if the old man had been rich, was just a vagrant, or was indeed an angel. If he was an angel, the boy was convinced that angels whistle when they walk."

With that, Judge Long presented David with the cardinal he had just carved during the story. David thanked him for it and asked if he could pay him something. "I reckon not," answered Judge Long. "Some things are worth less if you charge for it."

With that, David stuffed a dollar for the coffee in the honors cup on the counter and quietly left the store.

07

*I*nstead of putting the children on the bus, as usual, David loaded them in the car and took them to school. The little dog, Champ, needed his shots, and so the man decided he would carry the kids to school and then drop the dog off for a day at the vet's for shots and grooming. He would then drop by the old country store for a cup of coffee before returning home and beginning his day. Later, he would reverse course and pick up the dog and kids. *Besides*, the man thought, *Melba could use a little time to herself this morning. It must be tough on her with me or kids or the dog always under foot and her needing to look after us.*

The man gave each of the kids a big kiss and hug as he dropped them off, with Charlie being careful to make sure none of his friends were watching him. He was just too big for that now. Well, mostly. He liked the hugs and kisses from his dad; he just didn't want his friends watching.

After he dropped the children off at school, the man continued to the veterinary office and instructed the receptionist to give the little dog his six-month shots, then let the groomer cut his hair and give him a good bath.

David continued to the old country store and said hello to everyone. He poured a cup of coffee from the pot sitting on the old stove and began to listen to the talk from the old sages as they spun their tales.

As the man did that, Melba decided to take advantage of her free time without kids or dog or man underfoot and take a long, hot soak in the tub. The bathroom where Melba soaked had an interior door to her bedroom, but also had a door to the hallway that formed a dual entry. Melba was always cognizant of the propensity of little children to burst in on her at unexpected and inopportune moments, so she always made sure to lock the doors to her bedroom and the bathroom when they were in use.

Today was no different. Melba locked the door to her bedroom, undressed, and then carried a robe into the bathroom. She locked the door to the hallway as she ran the water into the tub, poured in the bubble bath and bath oils, and let the tub fill. She then eased into the tub and let the luxurious bubbles and oils caress her into a state of deep relaxation.

As she relaxed, she thought about her new little family, and how lucky she was to have them and to feel needed again. Melba exhaled and lay back into the water and enjoyed the relaxing warmth. She smiled to herself. Though she enjoyed her life here with the Wells family, there was never a dull moment—not with three kids and a dog to look after. It was just so good to have the morning to herself, she thought.

As Melba relaxed, she enjoyed the quiet of the house. She knew that soon Mr. Wells would be home. Though he would remain in his office working until lunch, he often worked through lunch, and she would bring him a quick sandwich to eat. Then, after school, the children would burst into the house, shattering the quiet with pent-up fervor. The house would mostly remain abustle until the kids were settled in bed for the evening. Yes, Melba loved all that and this new life, but she so looked forward to this morning of solitude and this soak.

As she enjoyed the warmth and softness of her bath, her ears perked. *Did I just hear something?* she thought. *No. It must have been my imagination.* She lay back and closed her eyes again. *No, there it is again—another bump!* Melba listened with a renewed interest. After a few seconds, she heard it again. *It's not Champ,* she thought. *He is still at the vet's. The children are at school. It can't be them. Maybe it's Mr. Wells. No, he said it would be closer to lunch before he made it home. Maybe he changed his mind?*

Then Melba's attention turned to the door to the bathroom. She heard a clumsy thud against it and saw a shadow pass underneath the door. This startled her. She knew this couldn't be David. He would never rap against the door in such a clumsy way. Besides, he would have knocked. No, this was someone else! A burglar, perhaps.

Melba quickly got out of the tub, grabbed her robe off the hook, and pressed her ear to the door to the hallway, listening intently. Yes! There was no mistake now. She could hear movement along the hallway! Melba's heart pounded. *What should I do?* she thought, as she listened intently to the sounds moving throughout the hallway on the other side of the door.

She ran into her bedroom where she quickly started to dress, listening to the haphazard noises of the intruder, and watching as the shadows occasionally went by the bottom crack of her doorway. She could only think to remain as quiet as possible. After all, the intruder didn't know she was there. But what should she do? She grabbed her cellphone from the nightstand beside her bed and called Mr. Wells.

"Hi Melba," the voice on the other end of the phone cheerfully answered. "I'm at Caughman's Store. Are you calling for me to pick up something? I'll be home soon."

"No! Shhh," Melba whispered in a terrified voice into the phone. "Listen, Mr. Wells, someone has broken into the house. I can hear them moving about. I can see their shadow. What should I do?"

"What? Melba, where are you?" David Wells asked excitedly.

"I'm locked in my bedroom. I don't think they know I'm here," Melba said in a whisper.

David Wells stood up from his place in the old rocker by the woodstove. The older gentlemen could see from his face and actions that something was wrong. They listened to the man intently.

"Melba, I want you to listen. Stay where you are. Keep the door locked and stay quiet. I will call the sheriff and I will be there in a couple of minutes. Just hang on!" said David Wells.

"Okay! Okay! But please hurry!" answered the woman in a quiet but excited tone.

"I'm calling the sheriff now, Melba! I'll be right there!" David Wells quickly dialed his cell phone as the other men in the store intently listened.

"Hello! Sheriff Johnson, this is David Wells. I just got a call from my housekeeper, Melba, that someone has broken into the house. She has barricaded herself in her bedroom. I don't think they are aware that she is there. She is being quiet so they don't know she is there. Huh? Yes, that's right, the old McEntyre place. I'll meet you there!"

With that, David Wells hung up his phone and started to quickly move towards the door. The four older men, who had been listening intently, quickly jumped up as well.

"We'll go with you!" Doc Holley said. All the men quickly followed David as he ran out the door, with Mac Caughman, the store owner, wearing his store apron, following the men into the parking lot. Each of the men jumped into his own vehicle, and they raced off down the road towards David Wells's home.

Mac stayed in the parking lot, and within a few seconds watched as Sheriff Johnson's vehicle passed Caughman's Store. It would soon overtake the caravan of vehicles that had just raced off.

As the crew reached the Wells's residence, the sheriff pulled into the drive as well. There, everyone jumped out of their vehicles, a couple of the older men pulling out the shotguns they often carried in the racks of their trucks, just in case the opportunity presented itself.

"You fellers wait here," said Sheriff Johnson to the group. "I'll call you if I need you. Deputy Grissom is on the way. He should be here any minute."

With that, Sheriff Johnson drew his pistol from his holster and carefully made his way to the front door. As he did, all the men waited in tense expectation.

When Sheriff Johnson made it to the front of the house, he stealthily began to peek into the front door and windows. After a few seconds of seeing nothing, he slowly turned the knob to the front door and made his way into the house, gun still drawn.

Minutes passed—minutes that seemed like an eternity to the waiting crew in the front yard as they listened for any sounds coming from the house. They heard nothing but silence.

Suddenly, Melba burst from the front door and frantically ran to the waiting crew. They surrounded her.

"Melba, are you okay?" asked David Wells.

"Yes, fine," she answered, still visibly upset.

"Sheriff Johnson, is he okay?" Judge Long asked Melba.

"I...I don't know. He knocked on the bedroom door and told me it was him. I opened it, and he whispered for me to get out of the house. I did. When I left, he was going up the hallway towards the noise. We could still hear them in there," explained Melba.

With that, the men turned their attention back toward the house, where they listened intently and waited for what seemed like an eternity, but what was, in reality, only a couple of minutes.

Then, as the men watched, they saw the doorknob of the front door begin to turn. Judge Long and Stan Nichols tightened their grips on their shotguns as they pointed them toward the door. Slowly, the door opened, and Sheriff Johnson appeared.

As he slowly walked toward the group, his face was stoic and expressionless.

"Wade, did you get him? Did you get the intruder?" asked Judge Long.

"Yes, I reckon I did," answered Sheriff Wade Johnson. "Tough old cuss though. It was a mighty battle. And he didn't want to give up easily. He kept fighting me. I finally won out though."

"Well, what happened? Did you have to shoot him?" asked Stan Nichols.

"No, I reckon not. That would have been a little drastic," answered the sheriff. "I just unhooked his battery."

With that, Sheriff Johnson pulled from behind his back one of the new automatic vacuums.

Melba looked confused. "What is that?" she asked.

"Oh, my!" David Wells exclaimed with a bewildered look. "You see, I got this in last night and hooked it up and was charging it and was going to surprise you today, Melba. But with the morning so busy and me taking the children to school and the dog to the vet, I guess I forgot to tell you about the vacuum. You work so hard, and I was just trying to save you some work."

The sheriff and the old men laughed, along with Melba and David Wells, after they overcame their embarrassment.

It was agreed between Melba and David Wells that the vacuum would be relegated to David's office room, and that Melba was quite capable of keeping the rest of the house clean.

Afterward, the old men would occasionally, and with good nature, refer to Melba as "Hoover" when she came into Caughman's Store, a name she accepted with a smile.

08

*D*avid Wells held out his hand, palm down. The dog, lying on the floor beside Stan Nichols noticed the gesture. The dog dutifully stood up and walked toward David, cheerfully wagging its tail because of the attention given. When the dog reached David, the dog nuzzled his hand and David scratched the dog behind its ear and then underneath its neck. The dog then sat down at David's feet, reveling in his newfound friend.

"What's his name?" David asked the older gentleman.

"*Her* name is Susie," the older man answered with emphasis.

David made a quick glance down at the dog in confirmation. "Her name! Yes. Excuse me. Hi, Susie," he said. With that, the dog wagged her tail even more rapidly and the young man scratched and petted her with added affection.

"But she'll answer to Sue as well, especially when hunting," Stan added.

"Hunting? What does she hunt?" asked David.

"Well, rabbits, mostly," the man answered, "but she has been known to hunt most anything she runs across. Rabbits, coons, deer.

But her specialty is rabbits. Yessir, nothing like hearing ol" Susie jump a rabbit and the rest of them dogs fall in behind."

"Sounds nice," David answered respectfully, noticing the blissfully happy and far-off look in the man's eyes as he spoke.

"Yep, I reckon there ain't much else like it," the man said. "Say, would you like to go sometime?"

Not wanting to seem rude, David Wells answered, "Sure," thinking this was some far-off invitation that would probably never come to fruition.

"Well, they are calling for frost on Thursday. They always run better after a good frost. How about then?" the older man asked.

At first, David was taken aback by the sudden invitation. However, he did want to fit in to this community and he enjoyed the company and conversations that the older men provided. He thought for a minute about his upcoming schedule and if he had any online meetings or had to meet in his office on that day.

"Yeah, Thursday will be fine," David answered. "I've never been rabbit hunting before. Do I need to bring a gun?"

"Well, no. I have an extra twelve-gauge you can borrow if you don't have one," the old man answered.

"Well, what time Thursday?" asked David.

"The earlier the better," the older man said. "But I guess we can meet at my house about 9:00. That way, you can get you some breakfast and get them young "uns of yours off to school and such. How about that?"

"That will be fine," David answered. "See you then." With that, they both drank another sip of coffee from their cups and enjoyed the warmth from the old woodstove nearby.

When Thursday came, David Wells quickly walked from the end of the driveway, where he waited on the school bus with the kids. Charlie made sure to hug and kiss his father goodbye before his friends could see. Anna and Beth, of course, still reveled in the love and affection exhibited to them by their father. They still needed that love and reassurance from the loss of their mother, less than a year removed.

As the bus pulled away, David waved goodbye as it disappeared into the distance, then quickly made his way up the drive for a final cup of coffee before joining Stan Nichols. He sipped on the coffee at the kitchen table, allowing the cup to warm his hands and soothe his mouth and throat with its warmth. Melba continued to clean the breakfast dishes she and the family had left earlier.

David explained to her that he didn't really know what time he would be home, but expected it would be around lunch. He looked down at his watch, took one final sip of that soothing cup of warmth, told Melba goodbye, and hurried out the door. Then he drove the mile or so to Stan Nichols's farmhouse, pulled up the long drive, parked, and ran up the steps onto the covered porch. Stan and his wife often sat there on the wooden rockers and waved as people went by, the cats flicking their tails rhythmically underneath the rockers as they seemingly slept.

David rapped his knuckles across the screen door and, momentarily, Stan Nichols appeared with Susie. She recognized her new friend immediately and wagged her tail, making loud thumps on the door frame. She sat down at David's feet to receive the scratches behind her ears and along the underside of her neck.

"Ready to go?" Stan Nichols questioned David.

"As ready as I'll ever be," David Wells said, trying not to appear too eager to the older gentleman.

In fact, David had been looking forward to this trip since Monday at Caughman's Store when Stan had invited him. David loved his newfound friends at the store and in the community, though the regulars at the store were considerably older than he was. But they had welcomed him into their fold easily, and he greatly valued their friendship and the stories they shared amongst themselves and with him.

Stan held out a brown hunting vest for David that had little loops on the chest with four shotgun shells on each side. The back of the vest formed a pouch to carry game. After he put the vest on, David thanked the older man, who then handed him a twelve-gauge shotgun.

David felt the shells hanging from the loops on the chest of his vest with his fingers.

"I reckon if we need more than eight shells apiece, we ain't doin" something right." The old man smiled.

The younger man returned a friendly smile at the older one, and they began to make their way down the steps.

"You ready to do some huntin', Susie?" the old man asked the small dog as they got out into the yard. With that, the dog's excitement level picked up along with her pace.

The air was brisk, and there was no wind, causing the frost to form a heavy white blanket over the grass in the yard. It almost resembled a snowfall. Susie quickly bounded back and forth ahead of the men as they walked into the side yard and toward the back of the house. As they walked, Susie smelled and explored everything of consequence, sneezing to clear her nose and take in the fresh, brisk smells of the cold fall air.

As they continued toward a kennel, consisting of a small building with a fenced outer yard, other dogs could hear Susie clearing her nose and came out of the kennel, barking welcome as she greeted them with her nose through the fence. The kennel was clean and well built, with wheat straw on the inside. There was even an electric heater hanging from the ceiling, which showed the great care given to these dogs.

When Stan reached the door of the kennel, the dogs within jumped on the door, wagging their tails. They waited impatiently for the older gentleman to lift the heavy barrel bolt on the door, slide it along its track, then slowly pull the sturdy door to the kennel open.

Once he did, the dogs made an orderly progression out of the kennel, each stopping at the feet of the old man to bask in his friendly caresses along their heads and shiny coats, as his soothing voice told them what good boys or girls they were. From there, they momentarily pressed their noses against the legs of David Wells, giving him a quick acknowledgment before quickly making their way to Susie.

Susie was the matriarch of the bunch. She was older, wiser, and more experienced, and each dog recognized Susie's place in the hierarchy of the pack. They had learned to hunt mostly by watching her.

In the spring, a couple of the mature female dogs would have a litter of puppies. The older gentleman would raise each litter, sometimes pulling a cord around the yard tied to a piece of rabbit fur from a previous hunt. The puppies would learn to recognize the scent, trail the piece of fur, then be rewarded with a piece of dog kibble, a scrap of bacon or ham, or some other piece of leftover meat from the previous night's supper.

The brood was then gradually sold off to other hunters during the year, or sometimes the next, as they developed their hunting prowess. Stan and his dogs were well-known and highly respected throughout the state, and indeed throughout the southeast. His reputation was one that he cared for his dogs, and they were of good quality.

Susie was mostly responsible for the training of the puppies. They would watch her and try to imitate her. When they would get out of line, Susie would bark or growl or sometimes provide a quick nip or a nudge. The puppies would be reminded and feel at ease with their place in the pack. It was the way of things; neither right nor wrong, just the way things were. The puppies, and indeed the rest of the pack, needed the structure of the pack, and Susie provided it.

David Wells watched as the dogs worked their way through the woods. The younger dogs worked quickly, running from one scent or one tree to the next, sometimes sneezing to clear their noses in the brisk air. Occasionally, one of the dogs would make a yipping sound or a small bark, and the other dogs would pause, then look to see if the dog had struck up anything of interest.

While the other dogs worked through the woods quickly, Susie was slow and more deliberate, taking her time and methodically analyzing every smell. Sometimes, the older dog would sneeze, clearing her nose of a previous smell. She would shake her head quickly, her ears forming a small windmill, then her keen nose snapped back to its work, analyzing the next smell.

Susie would periodically glance at her master as if to judge in which direction this hunt would take. The other dogs would keep their eyes on Susie for their direction. The older man was largely quiet, occasionally giving each dog a word of encouragement.

David Wells watched the old man and his dogs with keen interest as they worked their way along the small path through the woods. He thought about what a team that little crew made, how they all seemed to know their parts and depend on each other, and how the older man's eyes seemed to smile with pleasure as he watched his troop work its way through the woods.

Suddenly, the quiet of the woods was broken as Susie squealed. The other dogs paused in their tracks, quite still as they watched Suzie. Her tail began to wag more frantically, and her breathing intensified. As she continued to work, the other dogs joined her, trying to decipher for themselves exactly what Susie was telling them.

After perhaps twenty seconds or so of casting for direction, Susie's bark changed into more of a bay than the sharp yips as she struck the first scent. Then, Susie took off on a line, the other dogs falling closely behind, their noses to the ground and matching the deeper bays of Susie.

As the dogs took off hurriedly on their trail, David Wells took a few quick steps, as if to follow the dogs and their quarry. The older man, seeing what was happening, quickly placed his hands on David Wells's arm and quietly said, "Stay here. They've struck a rabbit, and he will make a big circle, if we are lucky, and they will all be back here d'rectly." David Wells nodded his acknowledgment to the older man, and they both listened to the bay of the dogs as they made their way through the woods.

The younger man had been so enchanted from watching the old

man and his dogs that he had taken very little notice of the surrounding woods. Perhaps thirty yards in front of them stood an old house. The darkness of the old, weathered wood causing the structure to blend into its surroundings. Most of the panes of windows had been long since removed, no doubt repurposed for other uses.

It was obvious to David that no one was living in the old house, nor had they for at least twenty years, perhaps much longer than that. A rusty, tin roof covered the structure. Though it looked as if it had been well-made, age and the elements had made the structure largely unsafe. The house was now slightly unlevel, as some of the older wooden pillars on which the house sat had either begun to rot or sink unevenly into the ground.

David couldn't help but wonder about the generations that had once lived in the house, how they had raised their families and lived out here in the woods and slow, easy country. Suddenly, David's attention switched from the house onto a large tree perhaps five yards in front of him. "Look," David motioned to the older man, "that tree is covered in nails, hundreds of them."

"That's a cottonwood tree. That tree reminds me of an old story I once heard, if you want to hear it," said the old man.

David nodded his head in the affirmative. Of course, he wanted to hear a story by the old man. The stories of the old men are what attracted David Wells to this community. It's why he made his way to Caughman's Store and the old woodstove there as often as possible.

As the dogs bayed off into the distance, David's attention turned to the old man.

"Well, you see, as I heard the story about an old cottonwood tree, much like this, there was a family that lived long ago, or so the story was. There was a mother and father that scratched a living from the soil and lived, though not easily as we think of the term today, but nonetheless quite happily.

"They had two children. The older son was strong and handsome and smart. He worked hard for his father and mother and spent long hours plowing the fields, tending the livestock, and doing chores probably too harsh in today's standards for any teen.

"The couple also had a younger son, of perhaps five or six, that was too young to join his father and brother in the fields. The two brothers loved each other. As time allowed, the older brother would take up as much time as he could with his younger brother, encouraging him and playing with him, talking to him, and befriending the younger sibling as much as possible. This was perhaps to ease the harsh, sometimes lonely, life of a farm child, often separated from the company of other children.

"And the younger boy idolized his older brother. He admired the strength and cleverness that he possessed. He wished more than anything that he could grow up to be just like him. The two spent every possible moment they could together. Sometimes they fed the animals kept near the house. Sometimes they fished together at the nearby creek. Often the older brother would read to his sibling a book about knights, or baseball, or some far-off land or adventure. The two adored each other.

"One day, the older brother didn't get up early, as was his normal routine. He remained in bed until the sun was well above the tall pines. Later, the older boy got up and resumed his chores, but he didn't appear as strong or as vibrant as the younger boy had always known. "Just a little cold," the older boy assured his family. "Tomorrow, I'll be good as new." And the next day he was better. He had his good days and his bad days, until the doctor was finally called.

"Though the younger brother couldn't understand everything, he knew it wasn't good news, from the hushed tones of his mother and father when they talked among themselves. He watched his Adonis of an older brother grow dark circles under his eyes and his body become frail and weak.

"The older brother continued to take the younger brother fishing at the creek, and read to him stories about far-off places, as his diminishing strength allowed, but those days became fewer and farther apart.

"One day, as the younger brother was playing by himself outside, he stopped his father and asked if the older brother was going to be okay. "You see that cottonwood tree there across the yard?" replied the father. "When the last bloom falls from that cottonwood tree, your brother will no longer be with us. He will have joined my father, your grandfather, in heaven, and he will no longer be with us.""

"The little boy looked at the wispy, cloud-like blossoms of the tall cottonwood tree in horror. *How could it be?* he thought to himself.

"The next day, in the early hours of the morning, the father headed out the door into the pale dawn sky, as was his custom. The little boy stood at the bedroom door of the older brother and watched him sleep in the semi-darkness of the early morning. He hugged his mother, and grabbed a biscuit left at the breakfast table by his father before he had made his way to the fields. Then the boy made his way to the barn. Finding a hammer and the large five gallon bucket of fencing nails, he stuffed as many into his pockets as space would allow. Then he headed across the yard and up into the branches of that majestic cottonwood tree.

"He began to hammer the fencing nails into the wispy blooms. There, he spent his days, hammering those nails, while his brother lay in bed and his mother and father did chores around the farm.

"But each day the soft breeze tore the blooms from the nails, and they floated across the landscape like passing clouds. Each day the little boy frantically nailed more and more blooms to the tree as his older brother grew weaker and more frail.

"Tears grew in the little boy's eyes as he fought against the inevitable to save his brother. It was these tear-filled eyes that caused the little boy to pierce his hand with a rusty nail. It was this that caused the infection to set in and the little boy's fever to mount. Soon, the little boy's fever caused sleep and delirium to set in. The doctor was called.

"For days, the little boy slept through his fever. When he woke, he looked for his older brother. When he went to his brother's room, the bed was empty. The little boy's mother and father explained to him that his brother was no longer.

"The little boy ran outside and looked at the tree through tear-filled eyes. All the blooms were gone. Left were hundreds of nails piercing the tree. Tears from the boy soaked the bark of the tree as he wept. Time and inevitability had beaten the little boy, despite the longings of his heart."

Suddenly, the older man shouted, "There he goes. Shoot!"

David Wells was still stunned from the story, but quickly turned toward where the older man had pointed and saw the rabbit running through the woods ahead. He pulled the trigger. The rabbit continued unhindered. Within seconds, Susie and the other dogs made their way along the scent trail left by the rabbit. They stopped, bewildered because there was no rabbit where David Wells had shot.

Confused, the dogs made their way to the two men. Stan leaned down to pet his dogs.

"I'm sorry," David said. "I guess I missed."

"That's all right," the older man answered. "The point of rabbit hunting never was to catch a rabbit, I reckon."

As the older man petted and rubbed his dogs, David noticed the time-worn scar across the man's hand. It was at that point that he realized the story the man had told him was more than just a story. It was a tale of life, and the tree covered in nails was a testament to the past.

The two men and the dogs largely walked in quiet as they made their way back through the woods. David watched as the old man carefully returned his dogs to their kennel, and he and Susie and David returned to the older man's house. There, David thanked the older man for taking him on his adventure. David quietly drove home, recalling his trip and the sight of the old cottonwood tree and the scar across the hand of the old man.

09

*D*avid Wells pulled the pillow over his head. The calamitous sounds of the children downstairs pierced the quiet of the morning, and David sought just another minute of refuge, another moment of silence before his body and mind had to face reality. Melba, the housekeeper, had the weekend off. She had travelled on a long overdue visit to see some of her family who lived out of town. Melba had been amazing over the last few months, taking care of the kids and the house. David was grateful to both Melba and Katherine for insisting on this arrangement. Even while sick in the hospital, she had provided for them, made a way to keep them moving forward.

David's eyes teared as he thought about Katherine's struggles in the hospital and how she just wanted to see that one last Christmas. Even through his misty eyes, David smiled. He smiled at all the good times he and Katherine and the kids shared. All the struggles in the hospital had been worth those moments, those memories.

Now, in the early hours of Saturday morning, the peace was shattered by the small troupe of his kids downstairs. In the background, David could hear the noise of the familiar Saturday morning cartoons. But it wasn't the cartoons that David's ears tuned in upon. It was the sound of little Charlie saying, "Gimme. Gimme." Then the lowered tones of Anna saying something, followed by Beth. Over and over this round robin of voices pierced the house from the bottom of the stairs and travelled up into David's bedroom.

David grudgingly pulled the pillow from over his head and listened to the kids shouting below. Even Champ the dog was joining in now, barking his own protestations. David then pulled the covers from his body, put his slippers on, and draped his robe over his pajamas as he made his way out of his bedroom and to the top of the stairs.

From there, he could see and hear the children more clearly. Anna was holding her hands, palm up, in the air over her head, as if she was some sort of waitress delivering a tray of food to a table. Little Charlie was in front of her, jumping in the air, screaming "Gimme, gimme."

Beth was beside Anna, the two of them laughing and shouting, "No, you can't have any, Charlie. Mmmm, these are sooo good!" Champ, the black cocker spaniel, was jumping into the air, as if he were after whatever it was that Anna was holding over her head.

David made his way to the bottom of the stairs and toward the children. He walked across the living room and commanded, "Hey, quiet down!" As he reached the children, he could see that Anna had nothing in her hands.

As he walked behind Charlie, he wrapped his arms around him and pulled him into his own body, as if half to comfort and half to help diffuse the war unfolding in front of him.

"What's going on, Charlie? Why are you screaming at the girls?" quizzed David.

"They baked cookies and won't give me any, that's what!" exclaimed Charlie as he stomped his feet and pursed his lips tightly into a giant pout. This set off another round of Charlie jumping up into the air, screaming "Gimme, gimme" to the girls. Champ the dog started jumping and barking. Anna and Beth were laughing and yelling, "No! We said you can't have any, Charlie!"

David looked bewildered. He said, "Okay, calm down, Charlie," and pulled him close to his body once again. He watched as Anna held one palm flat high into the air over her head, above Charlie's reach, and both she and Beth pretended to put something in their mouths.

They pretended to chew as they both said, "Mmmm. These are so good, Charlie." They started to laugh once again. This set off the protestations of little Charlie and the pup.

"Wait. What cookies?" the father asked. "I don't see any cookies."

"They are invisible cookies, Dad! And they won't give me any," yelled Charlie once again. "I've never had invisible cookies all my life."

Anna and Beth looked at each other once again and smiled as they took another invisible bite.

"And they are delicious, too!" laughed Anna.

Beth added, "Yes, delicious! Mmmmm."

"I see," said David. "Don't you girls want to share with your brother?"

"No, Dad," answered Anna. "He didn't help us bake them, so he can't have any."

"Besides," Beth chimed in, "Charlie got downstairs first today and got his cereal in his bowl and wanted to only watch the baby cartoons on TV and nothing we wanted to watch."

"They are *not* baby cartoons!" screamed Charlie as he pursed his lips once more, this time with fire in his eyes.

This set off another round of commotion with the kids and the dog.

David raised his voice above the ruckus. "Quiet!" he said, and the kids stopped. "I see. Are you sure you girls don't want to share with your brother?" he asked.

"No, Dad. He didn't help!" both girls protested.

"That's fine," the father answered. "Charlie, I saw that Melba left us the ingredients for some chocolate chip cookies in the kitchen for us to make this weekend while she was out of town. What do you say that you let the girls watch their cartoons on TV, and you and I can go into the kitchen and make our own cookies?"

"Okay, Dad!" said Charlie.

The girls" eyes stretched wide as they looked at each other, with bewildered looks on their faces, trying to fathom the turn of events.

"Okay, you girls go watch your cartoons while Charlie and I go bake some chocolate chip cookies," said the father.

With that, he grabbed Charlie's hand, and they and the little pup walked into the kitchen. Just before entering the kitchen, his hand in his father's, Charlie turned back toward the girls, smiled, and stuck out his tongue.

An hour or so later, David pulled the cookies from the oven and put them on a cooling rack. In a couple of minutes, He poured two glasses of milk and soon David and Charlie were sitting at the kitchen table, admiring the taste of the cookies.

"These sure are good cookies, Dad," Charlie exclaimed, as he took another bite and a big gulp of milk, forming a white moustache across his face. Then the little boy reached for another cookie and fed it to the little dog at his feet.

David looked at his little boy and smiled as he grabbed a napkin from the table and wiped the white moustache from his son's face.

"Charlie," David asked, "we have an awful lot of cookies. We'll never be able to eat all those cookies ourselves. What do you say that we see if your sisters want to share some of their cookies and we'll share ours?"

"That's great, Dad. But *only* if they share!" demanded the little boy.

"Well, let's just see," the man answered.

With that, the man got a tray out of the pantry. He poured two more glasses of milk, and placed them on the tray, along with his and his son's milk. He added the plate of cookies to the tray, then carried it into the living room. There, the two girls had been relegated to watching their own cartoons as they smelled the sweet aroma of the cookies wafting through the house.

The man set the tray down on the coffee table in front of the girls and they perked up, eyes widened once again.

"Charlie and I have a little deal for you girls, a trade, if you will. Charlie has decided he could spare some of his chocolate chip cookies and share them with you in exchange for some of those invisible cookies. What do you say, girls?" he asked.

"But only if they share!" Charlie demanded.

"Yes, only if you share," added the father.

Anna and Beth looked at each other for a moment and paused. Then they both smiled in agreement.

"Deal!" they both chimed in happily.

With that, the little family gathered in front of the TV. Anna and Beth offered the plate of invisible cookies to Charlie, then Charlie offered the plate of chocolate chip cookies to them.

After a bit of cartoons and milk and cookies, David looked at his children and smiled. "What do you think? Isn't it better to share?"

The girls reluctantly nodded in agreement as they took another chocolate chip cookie from the plate.

"Yes, Daddy," they both said.

"How about you, Charlie?" the father quizzed. "Isn't it better to share?"

"Yes, dad, but only…" Charlie's voice tailed off.

"But only what, Charlie?" asked the father.

"But only the invisible cookies are better," opined Charlie as he reached for two more cookies from the invisible tray, stuffing one into his mouth, and reaching down and feeding the other to Champ.

With that, Champ went over and smelled the little boy's hand, wagged his tail, then lay down in obvious agreement.

10

*D*avid Wells drew the warmth from the cup of coffee with his hands, then sipped, slowly tested, and then consumed the heated nectar. He watched as Judge Long pulled out a small pocketknife with a multitude of attachments, including a built-in compass in the handle, from his pocket. He then took a couple of pieces of mail from his inner jacket, and carefully opened the envelopes. He read the mail carefully before putting it back in his pocket.

"That's an interesting looking knife you have there," enquired David. "An antique?"

The judge laughed. "Well, I guess. An antique, just like me."

"I didn't mean to…" said David, in obvious embarrassment.

"Say I am old?" the judge laughed again.

"Yes. I mean, no. I mean—"

The judge interrupted once again with a laugh. "I know what you mean. Funny story about this knife, if you care to hear it," said the judge, as he scraped the knife across the top of his fingernails, then examined it as if he was in some far-off place and time.

"Yes, I would love to," answered David, always looking forward to their stories and wisdom.

"Well, funny thing about this old knife...it didn't always belong to me. You see, if you ever go walking way back in the woods where your property joins mine, you'll see an old farmhouse. I just use it for storage now, but it was where I grew up. And when I was born, I was born partially deaf. Everything sounded far off, like it was underwater or something. This caused me to have trouble speaking clearly. And that caused the kids around to laugh at me, treat me as mostly an outcast. My parents took me to a multitude of doctors and specialists, here and there, but they all said there was nothing that could be done."

"But you're a judge. You're so articulate. What happened?" inquired David.

"Well, you see, my speech problems didn't allow me many friends. I guess kids can be a little cruel at times, when they don't know any better."

David nodded his head in agreement as he listened to the judge.

"Well, you see, there was a family moved in as sharecroppers to the farm next door. I guess there aren't many sharecroppers today, but there used to be. The Mathis family. They were very poor. They lived back farther across the way in a little shack there.

"They had a son named Toby. Toby was what we called slow. Today, I guess they call it Down's Syndrome. None of that mattered to me. I was about six years old, and Toby about twelve. But we related just fine. He had a heart of gold, just as innocent and pure as you can imagine."

The judge laughed again. "Well, I guess we were both sort of outcasts to other kids, me with my hearing and speech, and Toby the way he was, other kids just laughed and made fun of us. I guess that was partly what drew us together. I was always at his house, or he at mine, or both of us in the woods, exploring and playing games. We were inseparable. We ate together at school, spent our recesses together, and became fast friends. I guess it didn't matter too much when the kids at school made fun of us. At least we had each other.

The judge paused a moment, and then looked as if he was in a far-off place once again. After a couple of seconds, he was drawn back into the present. "Oh, yes, you wanted to know about this knife," he said, as he scraped it against his cuticles.

"You see, I guess I couldn't have been more than six or seven. I had asked for several things for Christmas. One of those was this knife that I had seen a picture of in this catalog. Our house was decorated nicely for Christmas, and we had an abundance of presents under the tree, among them a small box. Oh, I was excited all right. I wanted that knife more than about anything, I guess. As I counted the days down to Christmas, I would shake that little box again and again."

The judge laughed. "My momma and daddy scolded me about it. They said I was going to wear a hole in that box shaking it so much.

"As school was released for Christmas, I was playing over at Toby's house, and we went inside for water. When I was inside, I was shocked to notice that there were no decorations, like at our house. It didn't smell of cinnamon or fruitcake, like our house did.

"Toby, where are your Christmas decorations?" I asked.

"Momma and Daddy said we don't have Christmas here on account of we don't have any money. Maybe someday we will, they say," answered Toby.

"Well, that certainly confused me. I thought Santa Claus just gave presents to every boy and girl. I didn't know that it sometimes depended on how much money your momma and daddy made.

"As the days made their way closer to Christmas, it worried me greatly about my friend Toby and his family. I certainly loved him like a brother. Besides, he was about the only one that could fully understand me with my lisp. He could understand me better than my own momma and daddy. I reckon he had some sort of gift for that.

"On Christmas Eve, I had asked my mother about Toby and his family and if Christmas was going to come to them or not.

"Well, that is the way of the world, I guess," Momma answered. "It can be cruel, for no good reason. Like you not having good hearing."

"But Christmas is Jesus's birthday. Won't he see that Toby and his family have Christmas?" I asked. "Even if I pray about it?"

"My momma looked at me. "Rupert, I don't know. I don't know what God waits on sometime. I've prayed about your hearing every single day since you were a baby, yet here you are, kids still making fun of you and nothing I can do about it."

"Except for my friend, Toby," I answered. "He doesn't make fun of me, and I don't make fun of him. Well, except when he put that blonde wig on at the store and told me he was going to grow up to be a movie star like some woman named Marisson Murlow or Superman or somebody like that."

"Yes, well, they say that God works in mysterious ways. I don't know. But it sure appears that he takes his own sweet time about things. I just don't know what he waits on," she said.

"She then kissed me on the forehead and told me goodnight. I couldn't sleep. I kept thinking about Toby and his family, and just didn't know what I could do about it.

"During the night, it started raining, really heavy. I lay there and listened to the rain. Sometime after midnight, I left the house and walked through the woods in the dark, held the fence wire up at the edge of the farm Toby's family was tending, then left one of those presents on the steps of Toby's house, along with a small note written on a scrap of paper, "To Toby, From Jesus."

"Before I got off the porch, the rain had turned into a thunderstorm, with terrible lightning, especially for late December. I took off running, back across their pasture.

"When I got to the fence wire, lightning struck an old tree there. All I saw was light and a loud sound. That's the last I remember.

"Sometime the next morning, my daddy found me there beside the fence, unconscious, soaked from head to foot, lying in a deep puddle of water. He grabbed me and shook me and patted my face and forehead and screamed at me to be all right.

"At first, it sounded as if his voice was far off, but it homed in as I came to. I could hear again. When I got home, Momma just held me and kissed me and cried and cried. As she did, we heard a knock at the door. It was Toby. He came over to show me the knife with the compass in the handle he got for Christmas and showed Momma the note. "To Toby, From Jesus."

"It's from Jesus!" Toby exclaimed. "I got a present from Jesus!"

"Momma looked at me as she realized where the knife had come from. I lowered my eyes, expecting to be scolded.

"Then I saw my momma, with tears in her eyes, smile. "Well, I guess we all got a present from Jesus this Christmas. Now why don't you go home and tell your momma and daddy that you all are invited over here for Sunday dinner, and I won't take no for an answer."

"With that Toby grabbed up his note and knife and put them in his pocket and went and got his momma and daddy and we all had Christmas dinner together, as we always did. Even after I went off to college and practiced law, we always had Christmas dinner together, no matter how far I had to travel.

"Over the years, Toby's parents passed away, and so did mine, and I moved back on the family farm to take care of Toby. When Toby died a few years ago, this is what he left me—this old knife, and that old scrap of paper. "To Toby, From Jesus.""

11

*M*elba was obviously a little perturbed as she walked from the kitchen and into the living room, where David and the kids were gathered around the TV, watching a movie. She placed both hands on her hips, as David looked up from the TV.

"Yes, Melba, what is it?" he questioned.

"Well, it's just that…" Melba paused as she contorted her face, "and I can't believe I did this. I simply can't believe it!"

"Yes? What is it, Melba?" David said as he sat up straight on the sofa.

"I can't believe I did that, that's all," Melba said in disgust.

David smiled and produced a small laugh. "What is it, Melba?"

"Well, I am baking a cake, a pound cake, tomorrow—well, two actually, one for the family, and one for the church picnic this Sunday. You see, Mrs. Jackson, down at the post office, gave me a recipe her sister Lavonia from Louisiana cut out of the *Women's Home Journal*, and I thought I would try it. But the thing is, I was checking my ingredients tonight, so I could get started early in the morning, and, well, I just don't have any vanilla extract. So, I was wondering if you would mind running down to Caughman's Store and getting me some tonight?" Melba asked.

"Well, Melba, I would be glad to, only they have already closed for tonight. But I'd be glad to go early in the morning, if that's okay?" said David.

"Yes, that will be fine," Melba answered, before returning to the kitchen.

"Uhmm, Dad? Can I go to Caughman's Store with you in the morning?" asked Charlie, eyes tenderly begging.

"Well, of course, Charlie! And maybe afterward we can go into town, and we can get an ice cream," answered David.

Hearing this, Anna and Beth replied in unison, "And me!"

David laughed. "Okay, we will make a morning of it then!"

The next morning, instead of the familiar Saturday morning cartoons, with the ensuing argument because Charlie was watching "cartoons for babies," as the girls liked to call them, David could hear the soft, quiet of cartoons playing, with no arguments. When David went downstairs to remind the kids to get ready, the girls were already putting on their shoes as they watched the cartoons they preferred.

"You girls ready?" asked David. "We need to get there and back so Melba can start her cakes."

"Yes, Dad. We are ready," the girls answered.

"And where is Charlie?" David asked.

"We don't know, Dad. He has been in the bathroom *all* morning!" Anna responded.

"That's strange," answered David. "I guess I should check on him."

With that, David headed upstairs and to the end of the hallway where the kids" bathrooms were. The bathroom door was closed, and David gave a quick knock.

"Charlie?" Are you ready?" he asked before turning the knob and peeking inside before walking in. There, he saw his son in dress pants and a white shirt and tie, dressed in his Sunday best, standing on a small stepstool, hair wet and slicked back, combing his hair.

Curious as to why his son would be dressing up to go to Caughman's Store on a Saturday morning, but not wanting to seem too curious and throw a wrench into whatever Charlie had on his mind, David decided to act nonchalant.

"Ready to go, Charlie?"

"Sure, Dad," answered Charlie.

David then gathered his three kids into his car and drove the young brood to Caughman's Store. Upon arriving, when the three kids got out of the vehicle, Charlie looked up at his father and said, "I want to stay out here, Dad."

Still curious as to what his son might be up to, but not wanting to interrupt his son's plans, answered, "Okay, Charlie."

Then David looked at his two girls. "Girls, I will only be in the store a couple of minutes. I want you two to stay out here and keep an eye on Charlie."

"Okay, Dad," they both answered. "And we can get ice cream after?"

"Yes, we can all get ice cream after. Just keep an eye on Charlie for a couple of minutes while I am in the store."

With that, David went into Caughman's Store and said a quick hello to Mac Caughman at the register. He then headed to the back of the store and said a quick hello to the older men who were sitting in their rockers and wooden-slat chairs.

David gave a quick look out the window to check on his children. As he looked out, he noticed Charlie making his way to the sidewalk in front of the store, followed closely by his two sisters. He noticed Charlie looking down the sidewalk at an approaching girl, about eight years old.

As the young girl walked close to Charlie, Charlie stood in front of her for a second. David watched as the two talked. David continued to watch with deep curiosity. Then, Charlie grabbed the girl, who was considerably larger than little Charlie, around the waist, strained his body, and picked her a couple of inches off the ground. As he did, the young girl coiled one arm up beside her body and hit Charlie in the face.

Charlie immediately dropped her and started crying. The young girl said something to Charlie, then returned in the direction in which she had come.

Anna and Beth rushed to their brother's side and started to console him, as David rushed out the door to his son's aid. As he made his way over to the parking lot, Anna and Beth gathered their little brother's hands and led him across the parking lot toward Caughman's Store.

David tried to take his son up into his arms to console him, but Charlie would have none of it. *Obviously, Charlie doesn't want everyone to see me holding him*, thought David.

"Okay, you guys come with me into the store while I pick up the vanilla extract for Melba. Then we will all go to get ice cream and I will find out what this was all about," said David.

With that, the father ushered the three children into the store and back to the grocery section where he found a bottle of vanilla extract. David then made his way to the front of the store, putting the bottle of extract on the counter, where Mac Caughman began to ring it up, casually talking to the girls and little Charlie, who was still sniffing with watery eyes and tear-covered cheeks. While the girls answered a cheerful "Fine, Mr. Mac" when he asked them how they were, Charlie could only muster a tearful sniffle. When Mac looked at David in a what's-going-on-with-Charlie sort of look, David could shrug his shoulders to signal to Mac that he had no idea what was going on with his son.

The group then gave a cheerful goodbye to Mac Caughman, before returning to the car—except for Charlie, who could only muster one more wet sniffle.

The group made their way into Crabapple and to Sweetie's Sweet Shop, where David ordered each of his crew a single scoop of their favorite ice cream, except for Charlie who preferred a small vanilla shake.

As they were all sitting in a booth, enjoying their special treats, David decided to mention the preceding turn of events.

Charlie's demeanor had cheered considerable as he slurped on the shake and ran his tongue along the straw each time he lifted it a few inches from the soda glass.

"So, Charlie, would you like to tell me what went on at Caughman's Store with that little girl now?" David asked his small son. "Who was that little girl anyway?"

"That girl? That is Mary Beth Lawton, Dad, and she is the prettiest girl in third grade, and she can beat all of those older boys at kickball at recess."

"Well, that's nice, Charlie, but what about what happened this morning?" inquired the father.

"Well, it started because she won't let me sit with her on the bus, Dad," said Charlie. "You see, she is also the prettiest girl in the whole elementary school."

Still confused, David inquired further. "I understand she is the prettiest girl in the whole elementary school, and that she can beat all the older boys at kickball, but what does that have to do with what happened today?"

"Well, you see, Dad, she said I was too young to sit with her on the bus, and the guys laughed at me. They said I was too young to pick up girls," Charlie said, as he ran his tongue along the straw, once again, gathering more of his shake.

David was curious as to where this story was going. "Okay, but I still don't understand what all that has to do with what happened this morning."

"Well, like I said, Dad, the guys teased me and said I was too young to pick up girls, and I said that I wasn't. Tommy Taylor even bet me a whole week of lunch money that I couldn't. And I knew that Mary Beth lives right down the road from Caughman's Store, and she goes there every Saturday morning, so that's when I did it."

David was confused one again. "Did what, Charlie? What did

you do to cause her to punch you in the eye and give you that great big shiner?"

"I know, Dad, ain't it a beauty?" said Charlie.

David laughed and ruffled his son's hair. "That it is, Charlie! That it is. But I still don't understand why she punched you."

"Well, Dad, when she came along this morning, I told her I was going to pick her up, and she told me that I wasn't. So, when I grabbed her by the waist and picked her up, that's when she did it. That's when she punched me."

David laughed inside at the folly of his son but dared not laugh out loud so as not to hurt Charlie's feelings because of his obvious misunderstanding.

"I see. So how was the shake, son?" he asked.

"Great, Dad" answered Charlie, as he slurped the last vestiges of his shake from the bottom of his glass.

"And how was the ice cream, girls?" he asked.

"Delicious, Dad," they each answered, in turn.

"Okay, great! Let's get the vanilla extract to Melba," David said to his children.

12

*D*avid Wells walked into Caughman's Store and went straight to the arrangement of rockers and wooden chairs that had become so familiar. He poured himself a cup of coffee and huddled near the woodstove. The older men who usually were here before him hadn't made it in yet, which sometimes happened when he dropped the children off at school instead of letting them take the bus. This was the last day before Christmas break, and they had presents they were going to give their teachers. David thought it best that he drop them off at school instead of risking those presents on the school bus.

It was strangely quiet in Caughman's Store that day. Not only was he not greeted by the crew surrounding the old woodstove, but Mac Caughman hadn't done his usual greeting from behind the counter at the front of the store as he walked in. *Well, sometimes Mac is in the back with stock*, thought David. *He'll be out in a moment.*

As David scanned the myriad of items in the old store, he caught the movement of a young woman in the back corner dusting the cans that neatly lined the shelves.

As he sipped carefully on the hot cup of coffee warming his hands, the woman turned and smiled. "Hello! I'm Angie. I haven't seen you in here before. I take it you live around here?" she asked.

"Yes. Hello, Angie. Nice to meet you. I'm David Wells. I live right down the road here," he said.

"Oh, yes. You built the nice house on the other side of Judge Long's place?" she asked.

"Yes. We moved in during the summer," David answered.

She smiled a big, friendly smile at David as she walked toward him. "Mind if I have a cup of coffee with you?" she asked as she made her way toward the coffee pot sitting on the stove.

"Not at all," answered David.

As she poured the coffee into a cup, David noticed her arms were covered with tattoos. She was pretty, perhaps twenty-five, not a great deal younger than he was, with long, dark hair that flowed over her shoulders and down her back. She seemed friendly enough, but the tattoos on her arms seemed oddly out of place for Crabapple Creek. It wasn't that David wasn't used to seeing tattoos on the arms of young women. He was from Atlanta, after all. It was just that to see that on someone here seemed oddly out of place.

"Well, I guess the guys are out either Christmas shopping or something, or maybe hunting. And Daddy should be in soon," she said, as she stirred cream into her coffee.

"Daddy?" David asked.

"Oh. Yes. I'm sorry. Mac Caughman. I'm Angie Caughman, and he is my father."

"I haven't seen you around here before," said David.

"Yes, well, I'm a veterinary student, and have been away at school. I am home for Christmas. I always come home to help out at the store and see everyone as often as I can," she said.

As she spoke, she took the coffee in her hand, turned to sit down in one of the rockers by David and noticed him staring at the tattoos over her arms. David knew that she had caught him looking at her tattoos, and he was embarrassed.

Angie noticed that he was embarrassed and smiled. "Don't be embarrassed. I know these are a little out of place for here."

"Yes, well, I still apologize for staring," answered David, his face red.

"Don't worry about it," she said with a friendly smile that disarmed David's embarrassment.

"So, you said you come back as often as you can. It must seem a little slow to you here, being away at college and all, and then coming back to this small community," David said.

She smiled a big smile at David. "Well, I assure you that there is no place else I would rather be. In fact, I'm going to be working at the vet's here in town as soon as I graduate in the spring," she said.

"Yes, I know, but someone your age, I would expect would just be itching to go out and see the world," said David.

Angie took a long sip of her coffee as she settled back in the rocker. "Well, let me tell you a story about a young girl that I once knew," she said, as she looked wistfully at the old calendar hanging on the wall beside the creamer and sugar and cups.

"You see, there was a young girl in high school, in a little community much like this one, where not a lot ever seemed to happen. Of course, being a high school student, she did want to see the world, and couldn't wait to get out. Her grades slipped. She got in trouble at school from time to time, and did all the other typical things that I guess a young high school girl might do.

"She deemed her parents too strict, too protective, not allowing her to do anything that she thought she was old enough to do. They weren't overly strict, just too protective, I guess. At least she deemed them so. She argued with them constantly, and just couldn't wait to get away from them...from them and that nowhere, square town in which she lived.

"One day, some of the kids that she went to school with were going to go to a rock concert in Atlanta. She asked her parents if she could go, and they said no, that she was too young to make a trip to Atlanta.

"She was furious. It was the last straw. She wanted to run her own life, to get away from that small town, her parents, and all the square and boring people in it. She made plans to run away. But where? Of course! She had heard about New York, that it was hip and progressive.

"But what of her parents? She knew they would track her down, if they could, and bring her back home. Her plan was to hitchhike toward Atlanta, then walk to a nearby town along the way, and catch a bus in the opposite direction to Charlotte. She would leave a bunch of literature about Miami Beach in her room when she left. That way, her parents, if they looked for her, would think she caught a bus in Atlanta and made her way to Miami Beach. *What a clever plan*, she thought.

"And, just like she thought, her parents searched for her and spent nights and weekends searching bus stations in just about every town and city from Atlanta to Miami, for any sort of clue as to their daughter's whereabouts. But she was clever. She had gone to a nearby town and caught a bus to Charlotte, even though it took most of the money she had to purchase the bus ticket.

"When she reached the bus station in Charlotte, it was the middle of the night. She walked out of the bus station, along the cold streets of Charlotte in winter, and found a small, all-night diner that was open.

"She sat down in the diner, looked in her pockets at the few dollars that she had left, and decided to just order a soda and a small order of fries. As she was sitting there, a big black man with a gold tooth and lots of muscles sat down in her booth.

"Hello, little girl," he said. "That ain't much to eat for a girl as big as you. Let me get you something."

"No, thanks," she answered. "I'm not hungry."

"The large man laughed a huge, friendly laugh. "Of course you are! Don't worry about me. I'm just here to help. Waitress! Get this little girl a big steak and a baked potato. And throw in one of them big salads you got, too!"

"No, really," she said, "I'm not—"

"He laughed that big, friendly laugh, once again. "Well, I've done ordered it now. I guess she'll just have to bring it. If you don't want it, it'll just have to go to waste."

"He smiled even more at the young girl. "Why don't you tell me a little about yourself? Are you from around here?"

"No, I'm from..." The girl's voice trailed off. "A different place, a small town." She realized she didn't want to reveal too much about herself, lest her parents would somehow find her. Besides, he was a stranger, and her parents had told her that she shouldn't talk to strangers.

"The man smiled at her and laughed. "Don't worry, little girl, I ain't telling nobody where you at. I'm just a friend, trying to help."

"The food soon came, and the girl's apprehensions about this huge stranger sitting in front of her soon faded. She ate the steak and potato and salad like she was ravenous. As she ate, she and the man talked.

"What's your name?" he asked. "They call me Brix."

"The girl paused, not wanting to reveal any more information than necessary. This man might tell the police and somehow allow her parents to track her down and bring her back home. Besides, she was a big girl now, a woman, and this running away wasn't so bad.

"The man laughed once again. "It's okay. You don't have to tell me nothing you don't want to tell me. Like I said, I'm just a friend trying to help."

"The girl and the man talked for a couple of hours in the small diner. Finally, the man paid the bill, and they both left the booth. They walked outside into the cold, wintry streets of Charlotte.

"You got a place to spend the night?" he asked.

"The girl poked her hand into the pockets of her blue jeans and felt the change and couple of dollars she had left. She had a blank look on her face, unsure how to answer.

"The man looked at her and replied, "Well, you can crash at my place for tonight, if you want to. Nobody will bother you there."

"Still unsure, but not wanting to face the cold, dark night walking the streets, the girl reluctantly agreed. They got into a big Cadillac parked in a parking lot next to the bus station, and drove to an old apartment building a few blocks away.

"They went upstairs and the man opened the door. There were two women there, and the sight of other women set the girl's fears at ease. "This is Claire, and this is Maxie," he said as he pointed at each of the women, and they said a cheerful hello. "And this is…" The man paused. "Well, she hasn't told me her name yet. But that's okay."

"The girl looked at the smiling man and the two women. Then, not wanting to seem rude, she told them all her first name. After all, it was just her first name, she thought. Besides, they had all told her their names. It would just be rude.

"They all talked about music and groups for a while, and Brix got some beers out of the refrigerator. The girl, not wanting to seem rude, drank a beer with her new friends. Besides, it was nothing that even the teenagers in her small town hadn't had before.

"The group soon pulled out joints and began to smoke them, but the girl refused. It was just a little more than she was willing to stray from the things her parents had taught her.

"Soon, the girl became sleepy, and Brix instructed the women to show the young girl to a bedroom. "Don't worry. No one will bother you in there, little girl," the man said. With that, the women showed the girl to a bedroom and closed the door behind as they left.

"The girl thought about how nice and helpful they all were, how they were looking out for her, how Brix had bought food for her, and provided a place for her to spend the night. This was nothing like she thought a big city would be. They were all so friendly. She looked at the clock and smiled. *Almost 3:00 in the morning! Boy, mom and dad would never allow this!* With that, the girl yawned sleepily and gave in to the heavy tug on her eyelids.

"It was the afternoon before she woke. She smiled as she looked at the clock. *Mom and Dad would never allow this! This is better than I thought!*

"The girl changed her clothes and hurried out of the bedroom and into the living room. Brix was talking on the phone. Soon, he hung up the phone and turned to the young girl. "Did you sleep good?" he asked.

"Yes," she answered sleepily. "I guess I was more tired than I thought."

Brix exploded with a big belly laugh. "I expect you was, little girl. You ain't used to this big city life. Stick around here and you will be a grown woman before you know it. Look, Claire and Maxie are still sleeping. Help yourself to whatever you like that's in the kitchen. I need to run out and check on some of my property. There's a shower in the bathroom at the end of the hall. Nobody will bother you there. I gotta go out now. We can go out for some more food when I get back. Talk at you then." With that, Brix left through the front door of the apartment.

"The girl looked around the apartment, which was still quiet because Claire and Maxie were not up yet, even though it was well into the afternoon now. She thought to herself, *Well, I guess it's a good time to get that shower.*

"She looked down the hallway and opened the first door slightly. There she could see Claire, lying on the bed, still asleep. Clothes were strewn around the room, over the floor, and across the bed and furniture so haphazardly that it really did look like a mini tornado had visited the room. The girl smiled as she thought of how her mom would have burst a blood vessel any time she saw her room half as bad as this.

"She slowly and quietly closed the door so that she wouldn't wake Claire. Then she quietly moved to the hallway to the next door and quietly peeked inside. The light from the hallway softly illuminated the bed and Maxie. Her room, too, was strewn with clothes all over the floor and furniture. The girl could see a mostly empty liquor bottle on the nightstand beside Maxie's bed. Once again, the girl quietly closed the door.

"She then opened the next door and saw a small bathroom and shower with bras and panties and clothes hanging from a makeshift clothesline. She smiled, thinking about how lucky she was to get away from that small town and parents who were always telling her what to do. Away from that small town filled with people who had probably never even seen a big city filled with the people that she had already seen. *This is the life*, she thought, and smiled once again.

"By the time she had finished her shower, Claire and Maxie were already up. They chatted a bit, and Claire commented that the young girl was pretty, but she would be even more appealing if she would put on more makeup. "You think so?" the young girl asked, as she turned her head to the side to give the two women a better look.

"We know so!" Claire and Maxie chimed in together. Soon, they were putting makeup on the teenager and doing her hair. The young girl enjoyed the attention and felt like these two women were her sisters—sisters that she had never had. By the time Brix came back, the young girl was thoroughly coated with makeup that made her look ten years older, though you could tell from her body build and facial features she was still a teen.

"Looks nice! You got potential, girl!" Brix smiled. "Claire, why don't you and Maxie go out and get this girl some clothes. That t-shirt and jeans just won't do. Makes her look too country. She's a big girl now." With that, Brix pulled out several hundred dollars from his wallet and gave it to Maxie.

"Oh, no, I couldn't," the young girl said. "You've been so good to me already. I just could—"

"Brix laughed. "Don't mention it, girl. I'm just trying to help. That's just what kind of man I am. Always looking to help."

"With that, Claire put her arm around the young girl. "It's okay. Let's go spend some of this money."

"The girl and the two women spent the rest of the afternoon shopping for clothes. The short skirts and tight blouses they helped the young girl pick out would have never been approved by her mother or her father. But they weren't around now. The young girl was now her own boss. She felt free—free and all grown up now. She thought of how much she liked where she was now and asked herself why it had taken so long for her to ditch her parents and all the people in that small town where she had grown up.

"The next couple of weeks saw the two women and Brix leave her alone in the evenings. She watched TV well into the night. She enjoyed her new freedom and being able to come and go just as she pleased. Claire and Maxie and Brix had been so very nice to her. Brix gave her money to spend each day, and Claire and Maxie looked out for her like she was a younger sister.

"A couple of weeks later, all that changed. Brix burst into her bedroom a little before noon. "Get your ass up, little girl. It's time for me to start getting some payback on my investment. I got a guy you need to meet. Don't worry. He's a good one for your first time. And I'll always be near if there is any trouble. I'll let Claire and Maxie stay outside your room for your first time. They will walk you through it. Or you can pay me all the money you owe me, and we'll call it square right now and you can be on your way. You do have all that money, don't you?"

"The little girl was shocked. This had all happened so fast. She was stunned, and didn't know what to say.

"Uh-huh. That's what I thought. Claire! Maxie! Get in here and get this girl ready! She's got bills to pay," shouted Brix.

"The little girl thought how Brix had been so friendly at the bus station that night, and how friendly Maxie and Claire had been. But he seemed so different now. Even though he laughed his infectious laugh and smiled that friendly smile, she could see something deep inside—sort of an evil, an evil that hid behind a mirror and in the shadows.

"Though the girl tried to remain tough and steadfast, she shook that first time. And Claire and Maxie waited outside to comfort her, as they hugged her through tears that she fought back.

"It's okay, dear," they assured her. "It will get easier. We promise." And they were right: it did get easier. But the girl knew that she had lost innocence that she could never get back.

"Brix was pleased with her. He was able to charge ten times normal because of her...innocence. He even gave the girl a fifty dollars bonus. Fifty dollars. *That's all it was worth*, she thought. *That's all I'm worth?* But she knew she had crossed some sort of threshold. He even had a tattoo with a brick and his name placed on the young girl, as he did with all his property. "So people will know you belong to me!" he said.

"And, in some ways, it did get easier. She found ways to think of other things as it happened, thoughts of her childhood, happy thoughts of growing up, her mom and dad and all the people back home. Things she used to curse under her breath, but now things she dearly wished she could have back. But she knew things had changed.

"So, she continued, made the best of her situation, and lived it up. But it was all on Brix. He paid for everything. He only doled out small amounts of cash to each of them, as needed. And if he found any of them trying to put money back, he confiscated it for safe keeping, he said.

"And so it was that the girl continued. Free. No pretenses. No getting up early to go to church with her family on Sunday mornings. None of the stuff that she always complained so bitterly about. It was just her now, and she was free.

"Months went by before she woke early one morning with a sickness. Her health had been going down, and she had dark circles under her eyes. She had gotten rail thin but now, if anything, she was gaining weight.

"When Brix noticed, he was furious. "I told you to be careful," he screamed. "Men don't like a girl with sickness. Claire and Maxie can take you to the doctor. He can take care of some stuff with a shot. And if it's something else, well, we can take care of that too."

"So, Claire and Maxie took the young girl to the doctor the next afternoon when they got up. They both waited in the waiting room, and sent the young girl into the cold, lonely room by herself. When the tests came back, they were all negative, except one—one that she wasn't expecting.

"When Brix found out, he screamed, "You ain't keeping it. I'll help you pay to get rid of it, but you can't keep it. I've got too much money invested in you."

"When the girl refused, Brix became even more angry, and physical. He hit and kicked the young girl in the stomach, slammed her up against the walls, and pushed her down the stairs to the apartment, trying to take care of the problem the young girl refused to let the doctor take care of in a different way.

"She finally relented, telling Brix that she would go to the doctor the next day to have it taken care of. Instead, she took what little money she had stashed away and bought a bus ticket to the nearest town near her home that had bus service. On the way, she used the burner phone that Brix had supplied all the girls working for him. She called home, again and again, but only got her parents" voicemail. She watched as the rain fell outside of the bus window and smoked the final cigarettes that she had left.

"She called again and again, without leaving a message. She didn't know what to say, even if they would have answered. The hopelessness in her heart was unbearable, like a weight resting on her chest, making every breath a crushing chore. *What if they don't want me back*, she thought. *How could they? I know I have disappointed them so. And now, this. What will they think? What will the entire town think? Maybe they won't come. Maybe it will be best. But, please, I have nothing else to do. I have nowhere else to turn.*

"Mile after lonely mile, the young girl watched as the cold rain pelted down on the windows of the bus, and the wiper blades pushed more off to the sides of the windows. Finally, in what must have been the sixth call—or was it the sixteenth, no matter, it was all a blur to the young girl—she left a message. "Mom, Dad, I will be at the bus station at about 2:30. If you could pick me up…" She paused. "If not, I don't blame you." With that, the young girl tearfully hung up the cheap burner phone and placed it back in her pocket in abject hopelessness.

"*What if they don't come?* she thought. *How could they? I am such a disappointment. I have let them down so much. How could they still love me? How could they have ever loved me? Oh, God, please help me! Please, someone help me!*

"The young girl decided that if her parents weren't at the bus station, she would buy another ticket for as far as her money would allow and keep riding.

"The young girl kept looking at the cold rain pelting down on the bus window for mile after agonizing mile. She was so ashamed of the things she had done, ashamed of how she had treated her parents.

"*They won't be there*, she thought. *They can't. Maybe I will hide in the back seat and not even get out. If the driver doesn't see me, maybe I can at least save the price of a bus ticket until the next stop.*

"*Oh, God, please! I can't do this!* Tears poured down her face as the bus pulled into the station, the cold rain still pelting down. She slowly stood up and stepped down into the parking lot, rain feeling so cold against her teary-hot face. Somehow, she managed to make her way inside the bus station, assured that her parents couldn't be there. Maybe that was how she garnered the strength to go inside, all but assured that she wouldn't have to face the disappointed looks on her parents" faces.

"Instead, as she stepped through the door, she saw a large sign with "Welcome Home" and her name on it. And then a cheer of "welcome home," in unison, as if at a birthday party. There she saw her parents with huge smiles and tears streaming down their faces. Her father, with huge, muscular, safe arms, wrapped her up and kissed her on the cheeks. Her smiling and weeping mother followed, and a doctor, and a judge, and a plant manager, and a farmer, and soda shop owner, and too many other people from her small town for her to name, all rushed and held her tight."

David Wells looked at the tattoos on the girl's arm. One was an image of a brick with "Brix" on it. Small writing that appeared to be added later said "Luke 15:11." Covering her arm was a tattoo of ivy that lay over the brick, as if ivy had mostly covered a wall. He then turned away so that the girl couldn't see the tears starting to pour down his face.

"I know it sounds like a sad story," she said. "But I want to assure you that it's not. It's one of the best, most happy stories imaginable." With that she gave David Wells a happy reassuring smile, and then turned to continue dusting the canned goods on the shelf behind her.

Just then, the front door opened, and McCoy walked in, carrying a little boy with skin noticeably darker than his or the young woman that David had been talking to. "We've been Christmas shopping," McCoy shouted with glee.

"Yes! Christmas shopping," the little boy cackled. "Christmas shopping for Mommy!"

David watched as the young girl ran to the front of the store, grabbing the little boy from the shoulders of McCoy, hugging him and kissing him, then doing the same to McCoy. With that, David Wells took a sip of coffee and felt the warmth of the old woodstove permeate his body as he listened to the cheerful noises coming from the front of the store.

13

*D*avid Wells watched as three older men held his kids on their laps, each of them talking and laughing with the kids. Each had a warm twinkle in his eyes. Stan Nichols had come in last, as he usually did, because he had more chores to tend to on his farm before he was free to join everyone else at Caughman's Store. This didn't, however, preclude him from purchasing suckers from the front of the store and distributing one to each of the children as he sat down on the chair at the end.

David smiled as he watched the men beam as they talked to his kids, and the children returned the warmth in kind. The men and their wives had practically adopted David's kids, and each became sort of surrogate grandparents to the kids. Both sets of the kids" grandparents lived on the west coast, so they didn't get to visit as often as they would have liked. However, the older men and their wives had grown to care for David's kids as if they really were their grandparents. David's kids had grown to love the older men as well. In fact, the kids had insisted on making or buying each of the men Christmas presents.

It wasn't just the men in the store. People at the little church they had been attending since they moved to Crabapple Creek had accepted them almost as family. However, none were as close to the kids as the four men sitting in these wooden rockers, huddling with his kids around the woodstove. Even Mac Caughman, upon seeing the kids, would usually grab a half gallon of milk and some chocolate, put it on a pot on the woodstove, and warm it for them whenever they came into the store during the cold weather. In fact, the kids were sipping on their hot chocolate now, and Charlie sported a tell-tale chocolate mustache.

After Melba had finished her shopping, she stopped by the woodstove to collect the kids.

"You kids ready to go?" she said. "I've got the stuff to bake some cookies for your teachers and Sunday school teachers at church."

"Okay," they all answered, as they hugged all four of the old men in turn.

"Well, let's clean you up a little bit, first, there, Charlie, before Melba stops letting you come talk to us anymore," Doc Holley chimed in as he reached for a napkin on the table.

"I'll do it myself," said Charlie, as he swiped the back of his hand across his face, erasing the chocolate moustache as he did. "I just want to do it myself."

"Well, why do you want to do it yourself?" asked Doc Holley.

"Well, it just tastes better that way. Besides, I get to lick the back of my hand on the ride home. Because once we get home Melba will make me wash my face and hands," answered Charlie, proudly.

Doc Holley laughed. "Good thinking there, Charlie." And all the men offered a little chuckle as Melba smiled.

The men helped the kids with their coats, bundled them tight, and said goodbye. Melba then led the kids to the front of the store, where Mac Caughman came from behind the counter and hugged each of the kids before they followed Melba out of the store, the squeaking screened door signaling their departure.

"So, you have the kids" Christmas presents all figured out?" Judge Long asked David.

"Well, pretty much—all except for Anna," answered David.

"Oh? And what is Miss Anna wanting that is so hard?" asked the judge.

"Well, she sees your horses, especially that little mare that you recently got, every time we drive by your place, Judge, and now she wants a horse," answered David.

"A horse, huh?" asked the judge. "Did I ever tell you that the first date me and Rachel ever went on was horseback riding?"

"No, what happened?" quizzed David.

"Oh, yes. But it was a terrible time though," answered the judge. "I'm surprised she would ever marry me after that little showing."

"Oh, really?" David asked.

"Yep, it was a terrible time. Why, I thoroughly embarrassed myself. In fact, I'm lucky to even be here," said the judge.

"Well, please go on, Judge. You have me fascinated," David said with wide eyes as he leaned in closer to the judge.

"You see," said the judge, "I thought Rachel was the most beautiful girl I had ever laid eyes on. Still do. But, you see, I was shy, and it took me quite a bit of time to work up the courage to ask her out. I mean, how could a beautiful girl like that take up with someone like me?

"Well, anyway, I had seen Rachel horseback riding, so I knew she liked it. Myself, I had never gone horseback riding before, but I was willing to take a chance, just to be near a beautiful girl like that, so I asked her. And, to my surprise, she accepted.

"Well, I was nervous, having never ridden a horse. I helped Rachel on hers, then climbed up on mine. Well, when I got up there, my horse took off! And I fell off the horse, and onto the ground, but my foot was caught in the stirrup. The horse kept galloping away, with my foot held tight in that stirrup."

David's eyes were wide as he leaned in and gasped at the judge's story.

"The horse was galloping, and my head and shoulders were bouncing over the ground. I kept yelling and yelling for help. "Help! Help!" But no matter what I tried to free my foot, the horse kept galloping and I kept bouncing. On and on we went, with my foot trapped in that stirrup and head and shoulders bouncing along the ground, with me yelling for help every step of the way. I'm telling you, it was terrible!"

"Wow!" David exclaimed. "How on earth did you ever get out?"

"Well, you see," explained the judge, "it was about that time that old man Cochran, who was the manager of the Piggly Wiggly, rushed out of the store and unplugged that blamed horse! You see, I was only about four at the time."

With that, the other men who had been listening intently to the story burst into laughter. David Wells, of course, knew he had been had and joined in with the laughter, watching Judge Long smile and look at him, eyes twinkling.

Then Judge Long added, "As for little Miss Anna, if you will agree to it, you can tell her she can come over any time she likes and learn to look after that mare of mine, and maybe we can teach her to ride. And by that time, maybe you can make a better decision whether to give her a horse and it will give you some time to get you a pasture fixed up for horses, as well."

"Wow, Judge, that would be great. Thank you so much. You sure it won't be too much trouble?" asked David.

"No trouble at all. Besides, me and Rachel would love seeing Anna around the house more," answered the judge.

"Well, thank you so much, Judge," said David as he took another sip of warm coffee and slid back into his rocker next to the old woodstove.

14

avid Wells's hands shook as he left the meeting with Mr. Burrows. The news was almost too good to be true. It was like winning the lottery. Mr. Burrows had offered to buy David's company. He would buy it outright and David would make a huge profit. He knew his kids would be able to attend any college in the country, and they would be financially set. The company would, however, have to move to New York, where David would become the vice president of a new division. All his present employees would be guaranteed a job in the new company with a substantial raise. It was more than David could afford to pay them at his still small company.

Still, it left David with a feeling in the pit of his stomach as he thought about it and flew back to Atlanta. This meant his employees would have to pick up and move their families to New York as well. And David's own family had settled in nicely in Crabapple Creek. The kids had all made friends at their new school, and the men at Caughman's Store, as well as their wives, had adopted his family as part of their own. Church was the same way. David and the kids had never felt so much at home as they did now. In fact, even Melba seemed happy. Still, this opportunity was like winning the lottery. All his family's wants and needs would be provided for, and the future looked bright.

As David sat in the plane on the flight back to Atlanta, he still felt something in the pit in his stomach. How could he ask his employees to move their families? Heck, for that matter, how could he ask his own family to move again, after they had just settled into their new home in Crabapple Creek?

As David drifted between the excitement of the new financial opportunities for him and his employees and the reality of having to start a new life once again in New York, the choice seemed overwhelming to him. It was a choice that he really didn't want to make. He wanted to do the right thing for his employees and their families, as well as the right thing for his own family. The problem was he really didn't know what the right thing was. Logically, he should accept the offer. Still, there was more than money to consider. It was people's lives. But how could he turn down an offer like that?

As he watched the clouds pass below as he looked out the window of the plane for mile after mile, David formulated a plan. He would call a meeting of his employees when he got back to the office, explain the offer, and give his employees a couple of days to discuss it with their families, then vote on it later in the week. David would do the same with his own family. If there was a consensus, then the decision would be easy. He could let everyone else make the decision for him, and he wouldn't have to worry if he was doing the right thing or not.

When David arrived back in his office, he called a meeting and laid out the opportunity and facts to his staff. He asked them to talk it out amongst themselves and their families. Then they would take a vote and he would decide where to go from there.

The employees, just like David, were extremely excited for the pending opportunity. However, just like David, they knew that it would mean moving their entire families. They set up a meeting to vote later in the week and then give their recommendation as to the future of the company.

Later that day, when David made it home, he called the kids and Melba together to explain the situation. He asked them to think it over and tell him what they thought the next day.

This all seemed like a great plan to David. However, when he got everyone together the next night, things didn't go exactly as planned.

"Anna, let's hear your vote," he asked. "I know you really didn't want to leave your friends at school in Atlanta before we moved here. So, what do you think?"

"Well, Dad, that was earlier in the year when I was still a child. I've made new friends here now. And my teachers are great. And my Sunday School teacher and friends there. And Mr. Mac and Doc Holley and the guys down at the store. Plus, I have a new responsibility to take care of the mare at Judge Long's. But, Daddy, I know you will do what's best for us, and I will be happy with whatever you decide."

David smiled at his little girl and gave her a reassuring hug.

"What about you, Beth? What's your vote?" he asked.

"Well, Dad, I kinda wanted to be around to show all those boys at school that I could play baseball better than any of them. They keep saying that girls have to play with dolls and that I can't play baseball, especially that mean old Tommy Brockhurst that keeps pulling my pigtails. I'm gonna show him as soon as baseball starts in the spring. But, Dad, I will do whatever you say is best for us, and be happy with it," she said.

David Wells straightened his daughter's pigtails that hung out of the bottom of her baseball cap and gave her a big hug.

"Okay, Charlie, what about you?" he asked.

Charlie studied his father a minute as he thought. "Well, Dad, Mary Beth Lawton will finally sit by me on the bus, and she always wants to share her lunch with me. But, really, I have a new girlfriend now, Sue Ellen Wilson. She's already lost her baby teeth, on account of she got hit in the mouth with a swing on the playground. She sure is cute. She can whistle real good because she's missing those teeth. And I would hate to have to leave her at such a trying time. She needs me. But I reckon you will need me just as bad if you move to New York. So, whatever you say is what I will do."

David fought back a smile because he knew it wasn't a laughing matter to Charlie. "Thank you for being so unselfish, Charlie, to me and Sue Ellen Wilson." He then leaned down and hugged his son tightly.

"Okay, Melba, that leaves you. How do you vote?" he asked.

"Well, I've made plenty of friends here that I would hate to leave, but you and the kids are my family now. So, wherever you guys go, I will be happy," she said.

"Thank you, Melba. And you are indeed family, and we don't know whatever we would do without you," said David.

With that, David pulled them all in for a group hug.

"Now we just have to see what everyone says at the office tomorrow before I make a decision. But, for now, what about us all running out for some ice cream?"

The kids all screamed, "Yay!" Then they put on their winter coats and spent the evening at the ice cream shop in town.

The next day, David called a meeting at the office with all his staff. "Have you guys met and voted on whether we should accept the offer or whether we should keep things the way they are now?" he asked.

Tom Delaney stood up and cleared his throat. "Yes, David, we have. We met yesterday and discussed it out in the open, and then we all voted in secret. Margaret and I counted the votes, and then I was named to speak for the group."

"And?" quizzed David. "How did you decide?"

"Well, David, the vote was unanimous. Everyone voted the same. We all acknowledged that it was a great opportunity. But, likewise, we recognized that we would be leaving a lot behind as well. So, we agreed that whatever you thought would be best, we would accept and adhere to. We trust you and know that you have the best interest of everyone in mind, or else you would have never given us the opportunity to voice our concerns and vote on the matter."

"Well, I must say that you guys sure didn't make it any easier on me," said David. "But I do appreciate your vote of confidence in me. I know this is something you guys need to know as quickly as possible, so I will decide over Christmas, and let you guys know by the twenty-eighth. We will have a quick meeting that day, and you guys can take off till after the first of the year."

With that, David adjourned the meeting and wished them all a Merry Christmas as he handed each one an envelope with their Christmas bonuses.

David Wells was proud of his crew, but also disappointed that they didn't help make the decision for him.

The Wells family wrapped presents, had a Christmas Eve service at the little country church they attended, and the kids delivered presents to the men at Caughman's Store, as well as the people around town. Christmas came, and the kids got up early with wonder in their eyes. They celebrated a warm Christmas together. Still, David knew the deadline he had set to make a decision about whether to move everyone to New York was fast approaching. It was a decision he dreaded. He knew the opportunity, not just for him and his family, but for everyone.

That day after Christmas, it snowed. David woke up early the next morning, no closer to a decision than he had been when this all started two weeks ago. His heart was heavy with indecision. It was actually hard to breathe, the decision so crushing for him. He decided to go for a walk.

He walked along his drive and down by the little country road. He travelled past his property and along the edge of Judge Long's. From there, he could see the horses grazing in the pasture, along with the mare that Anna cared for. Then David turned and walked through the snowy woods, pondering the heaviness of the decision that lay before him.

It began to snow harder. The woods became so quiet that David thought he could hear the snowflakes falling through the limbs of the barren trees with a soft shushing sound, then lying gently on the snow-covered ground. It was all so quiet and peaceful as he sat down on a fallen log. He watched as a couple of squirrels played tag in the trees above, keeping an eye on him as they played.

Then, as he sat and pondered the decision before him, he realized it was the twenty-seventh of December, exactly one year since Katherine's death. He remembered how Katherine had pushed forward cheerfully through her operations and chemo for two years. He remembered how steadfast and determined she was to push through one more Christmas with the kids. He thought about how Katherine had secretly interviewed housekeepers and decided on Melba to help him and the kids after she was gone. He recalled how she wished that, somehow, he could find a way to move to a small town away from the city in order to raise the kids.

He also remembered how strong and cheerful Katherine always was, how courageous she was. Then he remembered looking at Katherine's lifeless body as she lay still in that hospital, exactly one year ago to the day, and he cried. Now, he had another decision to make, and he felt so alone. "Oh, God, my dear Katherine, I need you," he said, weeping. "You were always the strong one, the sure one. I don't know what to do. I wish you were here. I need you here. Please help me."

Then David remembered how he left Katherine's hospital room and her still body and stepped out into the hallway. He remembered how he watched the snow falling out of the window of that cold hallway, just like today, and saw that redbird clinging to the small ledge on the side of the building.

David heard a rustle in the leaves. He looked around, and his eyes caught motion—a bright red against the black limbs and white of the snow. The little bird scratched in the bushes then stepped out, looking at him. David smiled as he wiped the hot tears from his face. He knew.

Printed in the United States
by Baker & Taylor Publisher Services